I0671764

McKinnell is a top-tier storyteller. *Anarchy and Other Lies* reads like Pat Frank through the lens of Mike Judge.

—Connor de Bruler,
author of *Goodbye, Moonflower*

"A pungent story of innocence lost in a world gone badly wrong ... a treasure chest full of great phrases, observations and survival tips."

— Pete Peru,
author of *The Reeking Hegs*

Jesse McKinnell's novel, *Anarchy and Other Lies*, is immediate and vivid storytelling. An existential America is filled with left-behinders who queue for fresh food but survive on nacho Go-Bars. When a dulled man rebels against his empty life, the consequences are sharp and unexpected.

—M Verant,
author of *Power in the Age of Lies*
and The Culling Gods

"*Anarchy and Other Lies* presents the near future we all know is coming—the one in which bees are almost a thing of the past, news and toxicity alerts flash across the lenses of our electronic glasses, and ration stations are needed because droughts have killed off crops. Poised for beauty and bleakness, mendacity and madness, Jesse McKinnell delicately handles a misguided search for love and hope amidst the inevitable disorder of a crumbling world."

—Nathan Elias,
author of *The Reincarnations*

"Anarchy will mean something different to you from what it means to me. The very concept of anarchy is therefore anarchic, as Jesse McKinnell's book sets out to suggest. But can we believe in it, even if we do not agree on what it is? If our own personal coordinates, plotted on the axes of our domestic and professional existences, are clues to how we interpret any concept, then my own idea of anarchy will be initiated by The Sex Pistols of the late 1970s and re-examined now, on a fulcrum approximately mid-point between those terrifying boyhood memories of punks and a notional future in which I imagine this energetic and splenetic novel to be set. In a world in which a tomato will cost you $15, there is – perhaps – the predictable dystopic fear and loathing, which is set aside pettiness and the hopelessness that was explored by the Miserabilist Movement of the 1990s. Here, anarchy has a pedigree, and where joy is dampened, the tensions tauten."

—David Mathew,
author of *Nostalgia's Boat*

ANARCHY AND OTHER LIES

BY

JESSE MCKINNELL

MONTAG

First Montag Press E-Book and Paperback Original Edition November 2020

Copyright © 2020 by Jesse McKinnell

As the writer and creator of this story, Jesse McKinnell asserts the right to be identified as the author of this book.

Montag Press ISBN: 978-1-940233-82-6
Design © 2020 Amit Dey

Montag Press Team:
Cover: Rick Febre
Author Photo: Becky McKinnell
Editor: Charlie Franco

A Montag Press Book
www.montagpress.com
Montag Press
777 Morton Street, Unit B
San Francisco CA 94129 USA

Montag Press, the burning book with the hatchet cover, the skewed word mark and the portrayal of the long-suffering fireman mascot are trademarks of Montag Press.

Printed & Digitally Originated in the United States of America

10 9 8 7 6 5 4 3 2 1

To Piper,
What a mess everything is. We'll try to clean
it up a bit before shuffling out the door.

"All the world is rising
up like vomit. "

— Ezra Furman

Chapter One

Fishbowls

My phone vibrates, clattering across the desk in a spastic dance. I don't recognize the number on the screen. Reaching for it, I hesitate then decide it's better to watch its seizures, safely insulated from whoever is on the other side. Eventually, it comes to rest. My stomach flips as I wait to see if there is a final buzz indicating that someone left a message.

This is taking a long time. It's either a long message or nothing.

It's nothing.

Something on the left lens of my glasses distracts me. There's another flashing news icon. I'm tired of the news. It's all irrelevant to me. I touch the command prompt on the left side of the frame and the annoying blinking at first fades like its feelings were hurt by my disinterest and then reluctantly disappears.

Out of the corner of my eye, I see Milli stick her head over the cubicle wall. I wish she was shorter.

I don't know if she noticed that I noticed her little jack-in-the-box routine, so I turn my back to her and hope she'll go away.

Pretending to be busy, I open my phone, flicking through the home screen to check the LOVE app. There are no messages waiting for me.

"Hey, New Guy!"

I don't want to dignify that little pet name with a response, I've been here for almost six months already. I turn up the volume on my headphones, adding another layer of insulation to my little cocoon.

"Hey, Jake!" Milli pushes forward cheerily.

A shudder runs through my body as I exhale all the air out of my lungs, put the phone to sleep, slide it into my pocket, and pluck the earbuds out.

"Hi Mill, what's up?" I rotate my chair half around, forcing a thin smile. It's as rude as I dare be. She's nice but looking at her smiling face every day has become too much to handle.

"Did you bring lunch?"

I nod and motion towards a brown paper bag on my desktop. Inside is a Go-Bar. I think it's nacho flavored. I prefer the ranch flavor but there aren't many options available anymore.

"A Go-Bar?" Milli asks.

"Yeah. Nacho. It's all I have left"

"Lucky. I love Go-Bars. Even the nacho ones. They're much better than Power Pouches. I know they're supposed to be healthy, but the texture is gross."

I nod in agreement. Few things left on this planet are as unpleasant as Power Pouches. It's like someone put a Go-Bar in a blender, topped it off with toilet water, and crammed the whole thing into a palm-sized plastic diaper.

Go-Bars first turned up after a particularly bad drought killed off all the corn and wheat crops in the mid-West. Fortified with the essential vitamins and minerals one would expect in real food, I think they were designed to make sure an entire population didn't malnourish and die. What an embarrassment that would have been for someone who's supposed to be caring about such things.

For a while, there were two companies making similar products. One came in a sludgy pouch looking like non-dairy yogurt puke. After a few months the yogurt puke disappeared - its death a capitalistic success story, no doubt. Go-Bars tweaked their exact formulation of sodium-based seasoning, became cheaper and ubiquitous in every pantry – an essential element of the American diet.

"Anyways, I can't take another one of those for lunch," Milli says sticking her tongue out dramatically. "Nancy and I were thinking about heading over to the ration station to see if they have any of those smoothies left. I heard the new raspberries taste almost real."

That sounds like a lie.

As Milli jabbers on, I notice my chair slowly turning until I'm facing her, giving her my full attention. I need to stop being so damn polite.

All the fresh food funnels through the ration station. Some fake military guys with combat boots run it, their crew-cut heads filled with the helium of self-importance. I'd rather eat my nacho flavored sawdust than deal with their bullshit.

"Thanks, but I'm all set with my Go-Bar. Besides I've got too much to get to here anyway," I explain pointing over my shoulder at the computer with my thumb, doing my best to feign resignation. I'm not sure exactly why I feel obligated to keep up the auspices of these mundane interactions, but I do. No sense in uselessly antagonizing her, I guess. The social programming runs deeper than I care to admit.

"OK, well, we'll be leaving in about fifteen minutes if you change your mind," she says hopefully before mercifully dropping down below the wall. "By the way, did you see the news about Charlotte?" she asks popping back up into my line of sight.

I sigh loudly. "Uh yeah, it flashed across my lens."

"It was a good effort, I guess. Too bad they couldn't save at least one of them. My mom said bees were everywhere when she was a little kid. She said they used to kill them with this spray that would shoot out of a can. She said it would paralyze them, and she and her friends used to watch them twitch on the ground for fun! Can you imagine? Nowadays you'd get arrested for even talking about doing something like that." With the last sentence, her voice drops, and she looks around to see if anyone else was listening, spooking herself.

Charlotte was the last queen bee that scientists or biologists or whatever had stored up in some manmade habitat in Florida or somewhere. She'd become a national fascination with the press following her every bee fart and fretting over her every bee sneeze. They had been trying to artificially inseminate her with bee sperm, or whatever it is that shoots out of their little peckers, but Charlotte had been sick for weeks and nothing had been taking. A solemn talking head on the newsfeed this morning reported that she had finally died.

The problem as I understand it is, bees do not enjoy sex as much as humans enjoy killing bees. This seems to be a common problem for all the species living on this planet.

A headline passes through my glasses: "Charlotte Dead - Biologists Warn of Worsening Crop Insecurity." I let it pass without seeing more - seems self-explanatory.

I nod at Milli making sure she sees that I look sufficiently frowny then turn my back to her. I can feel her sad eyes burning into my neck until I hear her chair creak as she settles back down. That's better. I run my fingers across the trackpad and the computer screen springs back to life.

I am supposed to be working on the new line of three-pronged, silver-plated forks. I move around some pixels, slightly adjusting down the height of the salad forks. They looked better before, so I hit the undo command and lean back in my chair. This seems stupid. If all the bees are dead, what the fuck do people need silverware for? Is there even a market for pointy, metal sticks left? We don't make them sharp enough to be efficient weapons.

My boss, Drew, walks into the middle of the room. There is stress written all over his face. His glasses hang around his neck and he pinches the bridge of his nose with his thumb and forefinger working the skin back and forth.

"Uh, Team, can we all huddle up here for a second?" Drew forces a smile across his face and then drops into the nearest chair.

There are about a dozen people in the office today and they quietly form a loose circle around Drew as he leans back. With his glasses off, it's easier to read his eyes - they look tired. Apparently, I was right, more bad news.

Being right is exhausting.

There is some nervous chittering as people flip through the screens on their glasses aimlessly, waiting for Drew to say whatever it is he has to say.

"Would you all mind taking your glasses down?" he asks us, a nervous smile flitting across his lips. The rustling ceases as the group closes out of their browsers and lowers their frames around their necks. It's strange to see everyone's eyes, unclouded by electronic glass, focused and correctly dilated.

Drew surveys the crowd, clearly struggling with how to begin. "It's no secret that we've come to the silverware game at a tough time for the industry. Sales across the board have been sluggish."

I know how this goes. It was stupid of me to take this job in the first place. All I've been designing are expensive metal trinkets. Eventually even the rich were going to figure out that it is a waste of money buying sticks and scoops for food that comes pressed into squares, ergonomically designed to be eaten with hands. I fade in and out for the rest of his speech.

"...This is no one's fault..."

Kristine in accounting stares at her toes, doing her best impression of a sad lady. I notice she has pulled her phone out of her pocket and is thumbing across the screen hidden down by her waist while Drew continues to talk. Her eyebrows rise momentarily as she fights back a smile, sucking her lips in over her teeth. She looks like a shrunken head.

"...The work is as strong as ever..."

Milli looks at the guy who started last week openly hoping he will notice her. It's annoying to see others performing the opening sequences of this dance right in front of me. I doubt she refers to him as "Hey, New Guy."

"...Corporate synergy..."

I can't remember the new guy's name, but he picked a shitty time to leave his old job. I think he worked for a garbage company or something. I wonder if they're hiring to back-fill his old position. I probably should have paid more atten-tion when he was being introduced. There's always a future in garbage.

He watches Drew's every mannerism like a lost puppy, oblivious to Milli's pre-coital advances. His eyes look dewy and wet, like he might cry.

"...Best team I've ever worked with..."

The senior designer, Greg, is staring right through Drew's head. I think he's been here the longest out of everyone, including Drew. He looks violently angry. I guess he isn't ready for a life devoid of soup spoons and salad forks. I watch as his hand forms a tight fist, then loosens, then tightens again. I don't think he is mentally composing his resume. Maybe he is working through a stroke.

"...Boxes are in the break room..."

Greg's eyes cross for a brief second and he staggers, almost imperceptibly, before locking his knees and catching his balance. I think I'm the only person who noticed. His eyes are cloudy, and a little bit of foam has formed at the corner of his mouth. I can see his lips moving, ever so slightly, talking himself into or out of whatever horrible plan his failing brain is laying out.

Jarred by his sudden deep breathing, his glasses reflect the light in tiny rainbows as they bounce slowly around his neck. He looks like a man preparing for the most important moment of his life.

"...Turn in your keys at reception..."

As soon as the last syllable passes by Drew's lips, a phone flips through the air rotating five times before burying itself into his nose. There is a satisfying crunch and then a primal war cry from Greg as he explodes out of his locked knee standstill and follows the arc of his projectile phone with a cocked fist.

Drew deflects Greg's punch away from his face, taking it clumsily on his forehead. Greg howls as his knuckles crack on Drew's skull.

He only hesitates for a moment before swinging his other fist up in a tight uppercut. It finds a home squarely on Drew's chin, bloodying his mouth and rocking his head backwards. Holding his hands out in front of his face, Drew lets out a high-pitched shriek as he tumbles over the chair. A scarlet mustache has already pooled over his lips.

"LIAR! I'M NOT GOING TO BE ONE OF THEM!" Greg roars, as he kicks away Drew's fallen chair and delivers a flying knee drop deep into our boss's solar plexus.

Drew lets out a "whump" as air exits his lungs, flailing helplessly at his attacker. Fully mounted across his chest, Greg pins him under his weight and rains blows down across Drew's forehead and neck. I can see a large gash opening above his left eye.

With his remaining oxygen Drew manages to scream "HELP!" before shrinking back into a ball, trying desperately to weather Greg's barrage of fists and swears.

Drew is getting his ass kicked, and he probably deserves it. Greg has kids and a wife; this is good therapy for him. The thought occurs to me to move forward to help. It would be the right thing to do, especially in front of the women watching.

Greg screams in some primordial language and drops the point of his elbow into the middle of Drew's forehead.

Despite the pressures of heroism that my gender-expectations has placed upon me, my feet remain firmly planted on the carpet at an acceptable distance from the carnage.

Finally, the rest of the pack wakes up and moves in on Greg. Two of the IT guys grab his arms and attempt to drag him off Drew's increasingly tenderized meat face.

Greg doesn't come easily.

The one with short blond hair, I think his name is Tim, catches his foot on Drew's prone chair and loses his balance. Greg, still sitting atop Drew, takes advantage of the mistake, pulling him closer to take a bite out of Tim's ear. He rolls away from the fracas howling as Greg spits a bloody chunk of cartilage in the air and continues his assault.

I guess this job really is over. I wonder if they're going to arrange for a severance package or something. I wonder if Drew is getting a severance package. I move away from the fracas as the IT guys regroup and make another attempt to save Drew's life.

In the break room, I find the boxes Drew promised. They're cardboard and stacked upon each other. Someone had taken the time to assemble them so they aren't just flat sheets. It's a nice touch actually, I'm bad at origami. I pick up two boxes and quickly run through the checklist of belongings at my desk. I put one box back and head into the main room.

Greg is pinned down now, howling like a coyote with its foot caught in a bear trap. The two IT guys, including Tim sans ear and the new guy from the garbage company, struggle to hold onto him. They're yelling at Kristine to find a weapon or something.

I wonder if there is an ax by the fire door. Do they even have things like that in offices anymore or is that just an old movie trope? I can't remember if I've ever seen one around.

Milli kneels around Drew's head. He doesn't seem responsive. There is a lot of blood. It's all over everything - a real mess. Kristine yells something about a fishbowl and the new guy screams for her to "fucking get it already."

I don't need this in my life right now. I turn my back on the chaos and continue towards my desk.

Glass breaks loudly in the other room. I guess Kristine found the fishbowl. I wonder what they did with the fish. Those things aren't cheap.

My desk is bleaker than I thought. A whole box now seems a bit overzealous. I've been here for six months and managed to completely avoid any personal items. I drop the box on the ground and pull my wallet out of a drawer. I wonder if anyone would notice if I took the computer.

In the other room, Milli screams "OH MY GOD, HE'S WAKING UP! SOMEBODY DO SOMETHING!"

I unplug the computer from the monitor and stick it in my back pocket then pause to look around one last time. This was an OK job, I guess. At least as far as jobs go.

There's only one way out of here and it's back past that bloody mess. How can that comply with the fire code? I take a deep breath, flip the hood of my sweatshirt up, and move out of the row of cubicles.

Greg is still lying on the ground pinned under the guys from IT. He's awake but his head is bloody, and he doesn't look like much of a threat anymore.

Kristin sits on the ground holding Drew's hand, rubbing it as she talks to him in a low hurried voice. "It'll be OK. Everything will be OK. Just hang in there OK." Each time she finishes, she pauses for a breath then starts over. The repetition is annoying.

Milli sits on the other side of Drew with her phone to her ear, screaming at some authority figure on the other side about how they need to get over here as soon as possible. That her boss may be dead. Etc. Etc. Etc.

I lean in for a closer look. Drew's chest rises in ragged intervals. He's not dead. It seems irresponsible for Milli to be screaming that right by his head. That's probably an upsetting thing to hear when you're still alive.

Drew's face looks bad, his nose is out of place, it moved from the center of his head and crossed over his left eye. His lips are bloody balloons, and with his mouth slightly open I can see spiky white stubs where his teeth used to be. Both of his eyes are swollen shut.

I wonder if I should thank him for the opportunity or something. They say it's important not to burn bridges with former employers.

I inch closer and lightly tap his foot with my shoe. "Uh, Drew? I'm going to take off." I pause for a second searching for the right combination of words; something that seems important but not too mushy.

This is awkward.

Before I can continue, Milli starts shrieking at me "SHUT THE FUCK UP!!! HE'S FUCKING DEAD!!!" Her eyes close tightly and her fists clench into tight balls from the force of her scream.

Again, I don't think he's dead, but it seems like a bad idea to debate the point with her right now. My mouth closes with a click and I turn on my heel towards the door.

Milli is still shrieking at me about Drew. The sounds bounce off my back and fall to the floor without forming any words. She seems to be confused, like I'm responsible for any of this mess.

As I go down the stairs, I can hear a siren outside. I just want to go home. Nothing here is worth the hassle. I open the door on the second floor and wait until the footsteps on the stairwell subside. Once they're passed, I finish the last two sets of stairs, and then I'm outside.

The street is full of people wandering around aimlessly. They are the left-behinders, the forgotten, the "them" that

Greg was yelling about. They are an omnipresent part of life now. Unwashed with no direction, they hang around waiting for nothing, their numbers increasing steadily, it seems, by the week. Even in my work clothes, none of them notice as I move amongst the crowd.

It's fall and the wind has picked up. I pull on the drawstrings and tighten the hoodie around my face. A gust rushes up behind me, catches my sweatshirt, and I have the momentary feeling of weightlessness as it sails me through two steps. Leaves crunch under my feet and flitter past me carried by the breeze.

It's nice to be outside again. Maybe I can find a job where I'm outside all day. I think I would like that. I wish I had listened to which trash company that kid came from. I could do a job like that, riding around in a truck all day, throwing people's shit into the back. It's probably fun to play with the compactor. Designing silverware was bullshit. I should have known that before I started.

I wonder if it's hard to meet women if you work as a trash collector. There's probably a stereotype. It's probably a really shitty job when it rains. I wonder if people ever tip around Christmas. It seems like a job you should get tipped for. I've never tipped a garbage man before.

I look up and realize I've already walked almost 10 blocks. It's easy to get lost with the wind at your back. I turn and study the horizon. In the distance, my old office building looms over the street. Blue and red flashers reflect off the windows. An ambulance must be there now.

The crowd has thinned and I'm alone now, close to the river. I can tell by the smell. There's been heavy rain the past few days and whenever that happens the river smells like rotten eggs.

I make my way over a short hill and head down towards the water. The houses in this neighborhood are mostly abandoned. No one wants to live next to that smell.

There's an old cottage that sits about twenty feet back from the shore. The paint is peeling badly, and a piece of trim on the second floor hangs loosely over a window. It sways in the wind and bangs idly against the glass. Someone has spray-painted ABANDON HOPE in blocky neon orange letters over the front door. Not the work of one of America's greatest poets.

I move through the overgrown yard and take a seat on the steps of the front porch. I need someplace quiet to hang out for a while and let everything at my office cool down. Some of the floorboards have rotted making the journey across the deck treacherous.

When I was a kid, my little brother stepped through a rotten tread on our back stairs. The jagged step sliced him open from the bottom of his calf up to his knee. He screamed, not in pain, but from seeing his yellow, gloopy fat fall out of the cut. It looked like a can of condensed chicken noodle soup. He moved away from here after college. Which was a good decision, as far as I can tell, there is nothing that should tie anyone to this place anymore.

Life seems to operate arbitrarily, like a game show host spinning a wheel. Sometimes it lands on the rotten floorboard and you flay yourself open for the world to see. Sometimes it lands on a deranged co-worker and you get your face rearranged.

So far my wheel has mostly landed on the little black lines that separate the pie spaces of tragedy and triumph - every moment, every step, every decision, every time I cross the street is another opportunity for everything to go violently wrong. The stress of waiting for life to catch up with me is stifling. Sometimes I feel like putting my finger on the wheel and getting it over with. The anticipation of the end is the most painful part of the human experience.

Humanity's worst invention is the ticking clock. Humanity's best invention is the millions of ways to distract each other from ticking clocks.

The wind is blowing away from me across the water; it helps keep the smell to a tolerable level. The water is dark green and teeming with algae and bacteria is choking out anything which might have had an idea about living there aquatically. If I tried, I could probably make it across by walking on it.

Tracking my proximity to the river my glasses vibrate subtly, and a message pops up on the lens warning me that the water is potentially toxic. The alert is followed by a list of articles tracing the history of the pollution, cleanup efforts, and their ultimate abandonment. I choose not to peruse them.

A gust of wind blows through, picking up a pile of leaves and dumping them onto the river. They land in a heap without creating so much as a ripple in the Jell-o water.

To the left of the house, there is a bridge that crosses the river. It's about a football field away and has been closed to foot traffic ever since I can remember. At one point it was painted green but after years of neglect, the paint has bubbled, and large patches of rust stand out.

The road behind me is silent, devoid of cars. I settle in and watch the bridge slowly rot. It's the most dynamic thing in my view, more alive than the green river or the tree; leafless, preparing themselves for another trying winter.

My glasses vibrate again to warn me the bridge is structurally unstable and has been closed for twenty years. It is followed by a trail of articles for me to choose from. Apparently, a kid fell off it five years ago and drowned.

Movement catches my eye. On the opposite bank, a head exits from the trees and darts to the concrete footing on the embankment. I watch as a woman wearing jeans, a black sweatshirt, and a bandana over her face carefully negotiates the steep clay sides of the river, before disappearing down underneath the bridge.

After a minute she pops back out from under the steel structure and looks around. A shock of pink hair juts out from underneath the hood. She carefully tucks it into the hood before scrambling back up the embankment, vanishing into the woods again.

A charge runs through my body just watching her. I don't know what she did, but it seemed illegal. I spot more movement across the river, so I push against the wall of the house, trying to make myself as small and inconspicuous as possible. I can't pinpoint the impetus exactly, but it seems like a bad idea to let whoever is on the other side of the river know I'm watching them. The movement in the trees stops but I stay still, focused on the bridge, mesmerized by something more than me, something impossible to describe.

Somewhere in the background, I hear the wheel spinning incessantly, the flipper rattling against the pegs as the universe decides again what to do with me.

Without warning the ground around the pylon connecting the bridge to the land around the river surges upward, making a mist of the clay embankment. The sound follows quickly; an explosion followed by loud cracking as the steel I-beams holding the ancient treads together follows the embankment up, twisting in the air before splashing down into the green muck below where the river absorbs the steel, choking it down like an anaconda digesting a goat. I search the tree line but can't make out any trace of the woman with the pink hair.

The bridge makes another loud pop as a second pylon gives way under the stress created by the first's failure. Cracks creak along the steel treads across to the other side of the street. The entire structure pauses for a second teetering, weighing its options before giving up and plunging into the sludge.

A large piece of tar, the size of a van, follows the path of the bridge down the embankment. It looks like an enormous black snake, slithering through the underbrush.

A crowd of people has noticed the commotion and begin to gather at the edge of the river. I see them looking around, pointing, and shrugging. No one gestures towards the trees on the other side. I don't think anyone else saw the pink-haired girl.

A police car with sirens howling pulls into the group. Two officers exit out of its doors. Their guns are unholstered before their feet hit the ground. A pulse runs through the crowd as they react to the presence of the weapons. No one runs but I can tell even from a distance a few want to. One old man steps forward as if pushed forward by the group. I can see his arms swinging over his head as he recreates the bridge flexing to and fro before breaking and falling into the river.

The cops keep their guns drawn, muzzles pointed at the ground, while the man flails in front of them. From this distance, they look like clones. As they move around, I can't keep track of which is which. The old man's eyes bulge and glisten in the late afternoon sun. I bet he is sweating terribly.

Suddenly, it occurs to me that I should probably avoid being seen. I've been around a lot of drama today. There's too much to explain. No one believes in coincidence this much.

Getting on my hands and knees I crawl around the porch towards the door, staying just below the railing. The door is open a crack, so I pull it ajar just enough to slip inside. The house smells like the river with a healthy dose of piss. The drywall is broken in large patches. Someone came through and ripped out all the copper pipe and wiring.

There is more bright orange spray-painted above the fireplace: EVERYTHING IS FUCKED. I like the second verse better.

Carefully stepping around the broken floorboards, I find my way to an outside door that opens onto the side yard away from the commotion and the cops. A sharp gust rips through the trees and rattles the loose piece of trim, slamming it loudly against the side of the second story. I jump and add some giddy-up to my steps putting serious distance between me, the group, the cops, and their guns.

As the sun goes down the temperature drops. I tuck my hands into my sleeves and cinch the hoodie as tightly around my face as the drawstrings will allow. Leaves crunch loudly under my feet as I cross through the neighborhood's yards, passing more abandoned houses left to marinate in the stink of the river. Other Technicolor spray-painted messages of hope dot their peeling paint. I don't bother to stop and process any more of the poetry. Eventually, when there is enough distance between me and the bridge to form some semblance of plausible deniability, I make a sharp turn and head straight back onto Main Street.

Streetlights spasm to life, bathing the road in their dirty yellow light as new, different people milling around. This crowd is a mixture of left-behinders and workers like me, huddled in their respective groups smoking cigarettes and decompressing from a day's work.

I pass my old office. It looks empty. My glasses kick on with a news story about a brutal beating in that building today - an arrest has been made. I ignore it and keep going down the road. People become scarcer and the lights less reliably in working order.

The last rays of the sun mark the horizon above the trees. They wink for a moment and then fall down on someplace farther west, leaving me in the dark below the flickering neon glow. The chill in the air intensifies and I shiver through my thin hoodie, sweating on the inside. People on TV are always talking about how warm the earth is now, but I don't get it. Most nights I still feel cold as shit.

At the top of my street sits Mike Michaels' brick campaign headquarters. Lost in thought, I make the mistake of cutting the angle to my street too close to the building. A sensor hums and a nondescript, three-dimensional white face with slicked-back blond hair pops out of a red, white, and blue background. Its all-American blue eyes, programmed to look friendly and approachable, appear hollow and manic instead, like electronic holes. I can see them scanning the sidewalk desperately trying to track me in the dark. "My fellow American. This November you will have a choice..."

I break into a brief run to get out of the range of the sign's sensors, its urgent message about the future nipping at my heels, getting fainter as I put distance between us. I make another turn off Main Street and two blocks later I'm outside my apartment building.

The shades on the oversized first-floor picture window are up and the dying light outside on the sidewalk is supplemented by my neighbor's widescreen TV. Despite my best efforts, I notice him standing in front of the flickering box wearing nothing but a towel, slung low over his bony hips. On the screen, a woman in a cheerleader outfit spreads her legs suggestively while sitting on a bench in a crudely drawn gym.

My glasses spring to life again and helpfully identify the actress as Chastity Bottoms. A man standing in the corner of the screen mouths something and starts taking off his varsity jacket. She blows a bubble, laughs, and begins to peel her top away. My neighbor's towel falls to the floor, and I make haste up the stairs to my lonely second-floor squat.

The door's unlocked. If anyone's pathetic enough to want anything in here, who am I to try and stop them? The apartment is dark, hopeless, and cold. I flip on the kitchen light, but it doesn't help. Things haven't come very far since college. The furniture is drab and barely functional, a ragtag collection that I've put together from yard sales and stuff left out on the curb as trash.

I toss my phone across the scratched-up dining room table and pull a heavier jacket off the chair. Even inside I can't shake the cold. If a woman ever got this far into my life, surely my sad apartment with its tattered couch and beat-up appliances would repel her. Fortunately, this hypothesis has never been tested.

Through the floorboards, I faintly hear a woman screaming. I turn on my TV to drown out the sound. A news anchor with a serious face swims into focus. He's in the middle of a story about the bridge coming down. It all seems like very serious stuff. He is very serious. This is a serious situation. His disembodied head is boxed in by text flowing in every direction, barking misery, and bad news.

A hand floats out of the ether and touches the newsman's earpiece. The head frowns dramatically as he looks down away from the camera, digesting whatever the producer is pumping into his brain. "Now, folks, I'm being told we have a piece of eye-witness footage showing the bridge coming down and a possible suspect. We're going to play this for you first here on Action News Six."

His face fades into the corner and the screen is taken up by the rusty old bridge. The woman with the pink hair climbs out from under the stanchion. She pauses again and tucks the shock of electric hair back into her hood. My heart flutters. It's an unfamiliar feeling. I hope it's not a precursor to a heart attack.

I watch as she looks around, darts up the embankment, and into the trees. The camera bounces along tracing her path. She fades out of sight and the camera jumps, apparently startled by a loud roar as the bridge lifts momentarily into the air before sinking into the green sludge again. In the left corner, the anchorman shakes his head in disgust.

I don't feel disgusted.

My palms sweat. I wonder if they caught the pink-haired woman.

The camera bounces up and down as the cameraman adjusts his position. For a moment, I can see my pants and shoes before the angle pops back up to capture the rest of the bridge collapsing.

My mouth dries up, threatening to choke me on my tongue.

I take the glasses off and stick them in the fridge. I should have known better. These things are not designed with an off switch. I turn back to the TV and the talking head is full size again.

In the left corner above his shoulder is a blown-up picture of the pink-haired woman. The resolution is poor and with the bandana, it's hard to make out any of the details in her face. She seems average in every way, except for her hair and skill with explosives. "Police are actively searching for the woman in this video. If you have any information, please contact..." I shut the TV off before he can finish. They haven't caught her yet. That's something, at least, I guess. I don't need anything else hanging over my head.

With the TV off, the floor starts moaning again.

CHAPTER TWO

Low Calorie - High In Vitamins

My mouth tastes like hot garbage. I grapple for the phone on the side table and clumsily thumb across the home screen. It's 9:30 AM already. Sun struggles to stream in between the dark sheets I have covering the windows. My back aches from holding back pee all night. Maybe without a job or a reason to get up, I'm reverting to an animal state, beholden only to my biological imperatives.

The mattress is on the floor, it creaks as I roll off onto my knees and wrestle with gravity until it gives in and I'm standing upright. There is no window in the bathroom, so I have to turn on the light. The electric brilliance blinds me and I stumble into the vanity, catching it in the soft spot that connects my hip to my groin. I rub it absently as I relieve myself into the toilet. It smells pungent. My guess is that I haven't been drinking enough water.

I finish and flip the light off without washing my hands because this is my house and I make the rules. I collapse back into the blackness of my mattress. I close my eyes, but the sleep has worn off for good. My stomach rumbles in three successive waves – biological imperatives.

I grab my phone and head into the kitchen. In the cupboard is the open neon orange box of Nacho Go-Bars. My stomach grumbles again but in warning, not hunger. The only other thing in there is an open package of Power Flakes. They are supposed to be blueberry flavored but taste suspiciously similar to the Go-Bars. I think they're the sawdust that flies off after they harden the goo up and cut it into bars. Nothing goes to waste here.

My stomach grumbles again, this time I sense indifference, the gastric equivalent to shrugging shoulders. At least the flakes aren't nacho flavored. I take the box and cram a handful of the sawdust into my mouth. They somehow manage to both cut the roof of my mouth and gum up my teeth – the wonders of science.

In the fridge, I find an opened bottle of water. My glasses are still in there, flashing angrily. They don't like to be ignored or cold. I take the bottle and close the door then down another handful of flakes, using the water to wash the gunk out of my teeth. They are tolerable if you do it in quick succession, closing the loop.

It's strange to not have a purpose in a day. No school to attend and no job. I don't need to leave the apartment for anything. There is enough here to keep my guts from grumbling too loudly; there is a hole in the floor that connects to pipes that keep me from living in my own filth; there are enough video games and electronic distractions to keep me from wallowing in my own misery. I should probably go outside, at some point. Vitamin D is supposed to be good for your mood and your skin.

I settle into the torn-up couch and flick on the TV. It's still on the news. A weatherman stands in front of a pulsing map and points dramatically towards some clouds with lightning bolts and frowny faces falling out of them. He shows the five-day forecast.

Today is Thursday.

Today is a frowny day.

Today is also rations day down at the station. I guess that helps explain why the cupboard is so bare. Today is the only day of the week when they pass out anything more than Go-Bars and those smoothies Milli likes. For the past five years, all the food has been controlled by the government. They control every step - production, processing, and distribution. There is less variety now, but it is more predictable.

They start unloading the truck promptly at 11:00 AM. People begin lining up at least an hour early. Sometimes Drew would let the office out, but usually, we'd be stuck in the back of the line, left with the more undesirable scraps. Regardless it feels good to have something tangible to do, a task to accomplish for the day.

On the screen, the weatherman throws it back to the anchor. He's wearing his serious face again. "Two disturbing local stories have some people wondering if they are safe *anywhere*." The screen splits again. On one side I can watch the bridge collapse for the third time - on the other side, a stretcher pulls Drew out of the office into the back of an ambulance. Greg follows quickly behind in another ambulance, cuffed to the stretcher. I wonder where the video is of Greg attacking Drew. Somebody must have left their glasses on during that last meeting. Maybe it's too bloody.

As soon as the bridge hits the water, the video from my glasses zooms in on the pink-haired girl's face and freezes. They found a frame where the bandana had dropped below her chin.

As if answering my thoughts, the TV pipes up, "Action Center 6 has the exclusive uncensored security cam-video from inside the office attack. See it at ActionCenterSix.com or on our app. But we must warn you, the video is extremely graphic."

Next up is a door crack interview with Greg's wife.

No, he's never hit her or the kids.

No, he wasn't on any drugs.

No, he never exhibited any signs of rage.

I take another handful of flakes and force them through my teeth, down my throat, and into my gut. The anchor talks to me sternly about how serious both these situations are and how terrified people are of leaving their house. I process this thought through another handful of the blueberry nightmare.

The news team breaks for commercials. Mike Michaels, the guy from the hologram last night, stands before a tattered American flag, looking off in the distance.

"My fellow Americans. We have come to a critical juncture in our country's history. Resources are low. Normal, everyday

Americans don't have enough to get by. On November 7th vote for Mike Michaels. Once elected, I'll work hard to prioritize Americans. There isn't enough room on this planet for everyone, let's focus on us..."

I switch the TV off.

It's already past 10:00 AM. I should head down to the ration station to get in line. Maybe I'll have a chance of getting more than some stale corn or smushed berries. I'm still wearing the same clothes as yesterday. I don't think they smell. I suppose it doesn't really matter all that much if they do. I'm just going to be outside waiting in line.

I flick on my phone and check the LOVE app. It contains no messages for me. My love life feels like fishing with no bait. I slip the black hoodie back on and open the door. It feels odd leaving the house without glasses on. Standing in the doorframe I eye the refrigerator and pause for a second while considering its contents. The glasses have become a crutch - an annoying crutch - but one that pulls at me, nonetheless. Holding onto the door with my left hand, halfway out, I vacillate again, then force the rest of my body out of the apartment and into the hallway, shutting the door behind me.

It sounds like an avalanche is coming up the stairs towards my apartment. Craning my head around the corner, an oversized man with red hair and a walrus sized mustache explodes into view. He spots me and scowls.

"Are you Jake Anderson?" he huffs.

I open my mouth to lie, but he shakes his head and clears the last set of stairs in three long steps.

"Let me rephrase, son. Mr. Anderson, let's step back inside your apartment for a minute. I have a few questions for you."

He's wearing a white shirt with the sleeves rolled up to his elbows and dark green suspenders. His red hair is parted messily. Standing in the staircase he looks as big as a bear. He pulls a badge out of his pocket and flashes it quickly before herding me back inside my kitchen, closing the door behind us. Standing in the middle of the room with his hands on his hips, he surveys my meager belongings. He does not appear impressed.

"Son, you work at Delicious Design?"

I quickly formulate another lie, something about a case of mistaken identity, but before I can open my mouth, he shakes his head and says, "Again, let me rephrase; why did you leave the office so quickly yesterday and where did you go?"

I want to start over again with the easy questions, like what is my name and where did I work. He crosses his freckled arms across his massive chest and stares a hole through me.

"They fired us. All of us. So, I packed up my stuff and left. I went for a walk."

"Uh-huh. You decided it would be a nice time to go for a stroll while your boss is having his face turned into a hamburger?"

The question seems rhetorical, but he stares at me waiting for an answer.

"Yes," I concede.

"Uh-huh. And where did you go?"

He sees the lies swimming behind my eyes and answers for me. "Did you see anything interesting down by the river?"

"There seemed to be a lot of commotion." My voice sounds watery and weak.

The man purses his lips and squints at me skeptically. I do my best to keep my eyes on the floor and wait for this to be over. Finally, he breaks the silence.

"Do you live with anyone?"

It's the easiest question he's asked so far, and I jump at the chance to be truthful. "No, sir." The "sir" seems like a nice touch.

"You got a girlfriend?"

Again, "No."

"Boyfriend?"

I shake my head sheepishly.

"You got any sort of family nearby or friends to check up on you?"

"Not really. It's mostly just me."

He harrumphs audibly and uncrosses his arms. "That's fine. People you worked with felt your behavior was very strange yesterday, anti-social. There's a lot going on out there. The world's a dangerous place."

He eyes me and twitches his mustache. It moves underneath his nose like a broom. "We're done here. I'll let you get on about your day. I'm sure you have lots of plans." He turns and grabs the doorknob. "One last thing," he says over his shoulder. "Who're you going to vote for in the election?"

Caught off-guard, my mind races and then goes blank and I stammer, "Ahh, ahh, umm."

"Never mind," he says quickly, cutting me off. "Have a nice day Mr. Anderson." The door swings closed behind him, and I listen as the avalanche falls down the stairs again before crashing out the front door. A car door opens and closes on the street, then the rumble of a motor. Tension has stored itself in my neck and I take a deep breath, trying to calm my body.

I peek out the window and confirm that the coast is clear. I really need to get to the ration station before it closes so despite frayed nerves, I force myself down the stairs and out onto the street.

The shades on my neighbor's front bay window are fully drawn, their exhibition over apparently. The sun is bright but there is a sharp undercurrent to the air. A shiver runs up my back as I walk down the sidewalk moving from shadow to shadow.

People are already out on the street. They all seem aimless, moving slowly in small groups. In recent weeks my morning walk to work had been getting more crowded. Two left-behinders wearing old flannel and ratty looking jeans are sitting together on a stoop about a block above me. They're smoking cheap, small cigars and staring down the sidewalk as I approach. I feel naked without the glasses, so I take the phone out of my pocket and stare down at it in my palm pretending to be engrossed in something important.

"Hey buddy, you got any cigarettes? We're almost out." The taller one grins at me, his little cigar pressed carefully between his lips. It smells sweet. Smoke flows out of his nose and billows around his bald head as he talks.

"No, sorry, I don't smoke," I explain without breaking stride.

They both get up as soon as I pass the stoop and match my pace down the street.

"That's OK. You got any money?" he calls at my back. "We'll also accept money."

"No, sorry, I don't carry cash," I reply over my shoulder, walking as fast as I can without jogging. The cold feeling is gone, instead, a drop of panicky sweat runs down my spine and into my underwear.

"You keep apologizing. It's OK, you don't have to apologize to us. You got any food then? We also accept food." The hairs on the back of my neck are standing up. I don't want to turn around and lose the momentum I have built but his voice sounds close.

"No, sor..., no. No food. I was heading over to get in line at the ration station."

"Well then, what the fuck do you have that you can give us? What about that fucking phone?"

I'm almost to the end of my street, back to where it intersects with Main. I can see more foot traffic three blocks away. Without bothering to answer I break into a run, seeking the security of a herd. Behind me, I hear them laughing. I'm not good at running and my footsteps ring loudly as my shoes slap at the pavement like I'm wearing flippers.

It takes three blocks before the panic wears off and I'm out of breath, but I keep my head down and don't turn around until I'm safely in the intersection. They are still standing where I took off, laughing. The short one waves to me with the cigar between his fingers. I stuff my hands into my pockets and turn away, heading towards the ration station.

There is a line forming around the block, a pulsing mass of people, everyone existing in the sweet singularity of their personal technology bubble. If those two had followed me, they probably could have picked all the meat off my bones without anyone noticing.

Looking down at my phone I get in line. Everyone else waiting is wearing their glasses. Their eyes are glazed, not seeing anything beyond the opaque screens pumping electronic signals directly into their brains. It feels almost quaint to be using my phone again. Having to actually move your eyes and your hands to access the internet is maddeningly inefficient.

On both sides of the line, street people without ration credits angrily eye the row_of technology zombies. Moving amongst them in pairs is Mike Michaels' street team. Wearing all white, at least a dozen fresh-faced young men and women work over the crowd passing out fliers, stickers, and little chocolates with Mike's beaming face on the wrapper. The street people quickly drop the campaign propaganda on the ground and chew on the candy, sneering at the people in the middle who could afford the ration stipend.

Unlike everyone I passed in line, the street people are eager to make eye contact. Their numbers have swelled in recent months. When the rationing first started the stipends were handed out for free, but as food became scarcer the government required a matching contribution. The amount seems to go up almost every month. There aren't enough jobs anymore for everyone to afford the match, which is probably a good thing because there wouldn't be enough food to feed them anyway. Life is circular for a reason - problems like this tend to solve themselves.

My phone buzzes as the little screen in my hand screams a headline at me - "Experts Predict Global Famine Death Toll to Reach 50 Million by Year-End. China Promises to Put Nuclear Option on Table If the US Elects Michaels and Foreign Aid is Cut."

I've never seen actual physical evidence that a place called China exists. I X away from the headline and open the LOVE app again. Still no messages. I thumb through the profiles, starting with those nearest in proximity. The app flashes, there is a woman in front of me in line who is online too. The picture in her profile is pretty, she has auburn hair and a long straight nose that parts two deeply dimpled cheeks.

I use the nudge function in the app to see if she wants to private message. The screen stops and blinks letting me know she is considering my nudge. It blinks and blinks and blinks. I'm trying to remember exactly what I have on my profile. My armpits dampen. I think my picture looks nice. It's from a family party at our summer house on the coast. One of the last times everyone was around. I was behind the house on a rock with my cousins. The ocean is in the background. The sun is shining, and I smiled legitimately. It was the only picture I could find where I looked happy. The screen is still blinking.

Abruptly the screen stops, she's decided to ignore the nudge and move on. I look up the line, but I can't see faces. It's hard to tell who anyone is from behind while they are bundled up in their jackets. It's upsetting to acknowledge that her rejection flooded me with relief. Sighing I lock the phone as two guys dressed in fatigues and combat boots start flipping the locks on the front of the station.

The ration station is an old metal shipping container. Someone, without much consideration for aesthetics, took a cutting torch to the long side and slapped an aluminum sliding door into it. A truck driven by the National Guard comes in the morning and drops off whatever meager produce they were able to scrape off the government farms. Then these two massive guys with a heightened sense of self-importance sling it out to the huddled masses. Everyone is expected to take what you get.

The produce is not great. It never lasts. It rots in a few days. I think the best stuff is reserved for the girls willing to make eyes at the meatheads who hand it out. I make it a point not to argue or look disappointed. I'm not much of a chef anyway.

With a rattle, the aluminum door is pulled up and the line surges forward. Food is doled out in cardboard boxes, pre-portioned. An old lady is first in line, one of the soldiers scans the code on her phone and hands her a box. She takes it quickly under her arm and shuffles off without looking at anyone else in the line.

There are at least fifty people in front of me, but the line moves quickly. Everyone has become accustomed to being herded. There is no room in the ration line for anything except mild boredom and begrudging acceptance. At this point, even if I tried, I couldn't think of a real question I would ask of the soldiers.

When it's my turn the soldier who scans my phone is short with spiky blond hair and bad skin. He doesn't look a day over eighteen. He catches me staring at him and sneers. I take my phone back and look down. The other one is older and taller, his gray hair hacked into the same bad haircut. His jacket is unbuttoned, and I see his stomach hanging out over his waist. It represents an impressive commitment to maintaining a gut like that nowadays. A cigarette burns idly between his lips as he passes me a box. I take it without looking up, and mutter "thank you."

I move onto the sidewalk and do a quick inventory. There is a plastic package of assorted frozen berries, 2 sweet potatoes, 3 russet potatoes, 2 yellow onions, a lemon, and some kale or Swiss chard or something. They've been working this same stock of berries since the summer. They're inedible unless you blend them into a smoothie.

Up the street, people scurry back into their hiding holes clutching their boxes. There isn't anything for me to do except head back to my dumpy apartment. I check up and down the street, there's no sign of the two guys who hassled me on my way to the station.

I have enough money in my account to get by for at least a month, which is good because even the thought of trying to find another job right now is enough to make my pits sweaty. I wonder what it takes to join the National Guard. I could smoke cigarettes, get fat, and be hostile to people looking for food. I bet it doesn't even require a college degree.

I make sure to stay on the other side of the street, away from the campaign headquarters with the Michaels' hologram. Two teenagers holding hands get caught in its crazy-eyed tractor beam. They jump back startled as the dialogue rolls, "My fellow Americans..."

The boy stoops down, picks up a rock, and hurls it towards the apparition.

"This November you will have a choice..."

He spits on the ground and yells, "Fuck Off," before picking up another rock and letting it fly. This time it clatters against the equipment loudly and the signal flickers. He steps back and waits hopefully. The face flickers again and then strains forward, "My fellow Americans" resetting itself.

The boy yells something I can't make out and stoops down for another rock. The girl grabs him by the arm and runs a hand through the back of his hair, soothingly. He struggles for a second, then gives in and lets her guide him down the street.

"Vote for Mike Michaels because there isn't enough room for all of us anymore." The words fall at the couple's heels.

I turn left and drop in behind the row of apartment houses on my street. There is only one way in and out. If those two bums are waiting for me there is no way to avoid them on the road. I keep my head down and hurry along the last few blocks towards my little shithole. My neighbors' fences are too high, and I switch back onto the street to finish the journey.

"Hey Buddy, whatcha got?"

The question startles me. The two bums from earlier materialize out of thin air and fall in behind me again.

The tall, bald one nods at the box under my arm, "You were in quite a hurry this morning. What'd they have today?"

I shift the box to my other arm and try to summon up enough spit to answer. "Nothing good," I squeak out trying to smile.

"Yeah, typical, right?" the tall one replies, grinning widely. "We had to trade our rations for these." He holds up the pack of cigars.

I feel like a lonely zebra, lost in the Serengeti, negotiating with lions.

"Did you get enough to share?" the short one asks. He's short and wide with miskempt brown hair. A week's worth of dirty beard juts out from his cheeks. His eyes are baby blue, so much so that some poor girl probably fell in love with them somewhere along the line. Life and time have turned them cloudy and dull, the whites now tinted with a greenish hue. He grins at me feigning innocence, awaiting my response.

I look at my meager box and inventory it again. There is nothing in there worth defending. There will be more rations next week. I'll just take a different route in the future.

"Take it," I concede, handing the box to the tall one.

He clucks his tongue, "Ahh really? That's awfully generous." He yanks the box from my hands, looks inside, and smiles. "They got no problems growing potatoes."

The shorter one laughs and takes a deep drag from his cigar. Smoke billows from his nose and suspends in the crisp autumn air. The two stand there staring at me, un-bothered by the heist they just committed.

I can't think of anything to say, so I stick my empty hands into my pockets and slide past them down the street towards my apartment. Their laughter trails after me. They probably wouldn't have tried this bullshit if I was wearing my glasses. It was stupid to leave the house without them. There is a glowing red target on my back.

I could report them to the cops but I guess they didn't really commit a crime. Maybe I should have taken the beating. I could probably go on disability or something if I had.

My phone vibrates in my pocket, so I take it out to see if someone is nudge-ing me on LOVE. It's an email from Delicious Design updating us former staff on Drew's condition. Apparently, he's breathing on his own now but is being kept in a medically induced coma for precautionary reasons. The email makes no mention of Greg. I wonder how he's doing after taking a fishbowl to the skull.

My neighbor's shades are wide open again. I close my eyes, fumble for the doorknob, find it, and escape up the stairs.

CHAPTER THREE

What Did You Do To Harry?

I made the decision not to leave my house again, maybe forever. There isn't any reason to venture outside. For a week I keep the shades drawn. If it wasn't for the clocks on my phone, the TV, and my glasses, I would have no conception on when it was daylight and when it was night.

I keep myself distracted with a constant barrage of video games. I've found that my brain, despite its protestations to the contrary, is a very simple machine to manipulate. By feeding it a steady diet of simulated violence, I have been able to retrain it from being a worry machine into an endorphin vending machine.

Feeling glum? Chainsaw some zombies.

Anxious about the future? Take sniper shots at Nazis.

Struggling with self-esteem? Beat some street thugs to death with a barbed-wire covered baseball bat.

I commit to a diet of three Go-Bars a day, water, handfuls of Power Flakes, and glowing screens to make the time pass in tolerable intervals. While coming down from the highs of simulated violence, I reach out to five different women on LOVE. None of them accept my nudge and message me back. Hours pass looking for that pink-haired woman online, but there is no trace of her beyond the video my glasses took.

For the first few days, there is plenty of news coverage about the bridge. The police don't seem to have any real leads, so it dies down towards the end of the week. The news cycle is dominated by the presidential election. I do my best to ignore all of it.

When my brain starts to make things complicated, I shove more video games into it. I leveled up three times on DRONE, enough to jump my ranking into Blue Squadron, representing the top thirty percent of players currently. I pushed myself hard to get there. So much time spent flying the black buzzing box, evading enemy fire, and dropping cluster bombs into tight target boxes has left me feeling nauseated.

The top one percent of DRONE players have professional contracts with the military to run glamorous bombing missions against high-priority targets. They make more money than I could ever spend on Go-Bars. I'm still stuck running simulations and patrols for free in a low-stakes desert environment.

I got another email from Delicious Design. Drew is awake and everyone is optimistic that eventually, he will regain control of his bodily functions. Right now, apparently, he has to pee through a tube and poop into some sort of tub.

The emails are very specific.

There doesn't appear to be any way to "unsubscribe" from these updates, and it's easier to ignore them than to email whoever is on the other side and tell them to knock it off. The updates still make no mention of Greg. There was a brief item on the news one night that he's in the hospital too and is under psychiatric evaluation. The anchor gravely told me the police have yet to press charges.

It is rations day again. My phone vibrates with a notification that my option to purchase this week's box is available. Remembering the two thugs who grafted my shit last week, my thumb hesitates over the Accept button. A week of being stuck inside with nothing but simulated violence and simulated food has left me punchy and bloated. I'm afraid of what will happen if I spend another week holed up in here. A trip to the ration station seems like an appropriate excuse to end my isolation.

All the Go-Bars are giving me the runs anyway. They're high in fiber and made to be easily digestible. I tap the Accept button and a scannable coupon pops up.

Toggling through my phone, I check my account balance; there is a little over three months' worth of rent and rations left in my account. I should leave a buffer in case I can't find a job right away.

I pull back one of the coverings on the window. Outside is gray and harsh looking. There is a steady drizzle slowly filling up the puddles along the street. I strain my neck down the sidewalk. No one is outside. Those two cretins are probably holed up somewhere eating the last of my yams.

I think about that woman in line last week who ignored my nudges on LOVE. I look like microwaved crap and smell even worse. If I just let it go, maybe someday I can be the guy who robs idiots of their ration boxes.

Society is based around sex; it provides the impetus to look and smell as presentable as possible. It's held out like a carrot in front of a starving donkey, urging the beast ever onward, never acknowledging how unattainable it really is. In order to get sex, we follow the rules, we go to work to earn money, there we are productive and if we're good or lucky, we meet someone special who touches us in peculiar but specific ways and the world keeps spinning. I've already lost my job; I already smell like shit. If I can manage to shake the illusion of sex, I can let this apartment go and perhaps pursue a life of purpose or crime instead.

I consider my options.

I would have to become a lot tougher in order to have the confidence to rob even the most useless pile of white paste, like myself. Becoming an expert on tough would take quite a few ass-kickings. Living a life of purpose would require some sort of calling or skill and years of tireless devotion. On the other hand, I can take a hot shower and continue to hopelessly chase orgasms that I don't initiate on my own.

Never changing is always the easiest option.

I sigh and go around the apartment opening the blinds on all the windows. The outside bathes my meager belongings in dirty dishwater light. Looking around at the mess I've made over the past week of isolation makes me even more depressed.

I turn on the shower and crank the handle all the way around, opening the tap as hot as possible and step in. The water scalds me. I hold steady under the flow and after a few seconds, my skin turns lobster red.

As the water runs, I take inventory of where my week of sloth has led me. Except for where the water has burned me, my skin is pale white, dotted with random splotches of dark black hair. There is no rhyme or reason or manliness to my mane. Instead, it looks like a postmodern splatter painter used my carcass as a canvas.

My stomach sticks out a bit further than my chest. Jabbing a finger into the bellybutton causes the flesh to easily give way. It feels like if I tried, I could push all the way into my internal organs. This is not my best selling point for a woman.

Out of the shower, I slip on clean underwear and stand in front of the mirror again. I suck my gut in as far as possible and flex my arms. My skin barely moves, apparently agnostic as to the presence of any muscles lurking underneath. This is the body of a man built for leisure. I release the breath I was holding and my gut rolls back into place.

Life never ceases to discourage.

Squatting down, I labor through ten shaky pushups, then pop back up into view of the mirror to check for results. My chest is flushed red, rising, and falling rapidly. My armpits are on the edge of releasing a torrent of sweat to put out the fire this bit of exercise has sent raging through my torso. Other than that, nothing.

Back down on the ground, I grunt out twenty sit-ups, cheating through the last five. Beads of sweat pop out on my brow. Standing up in front of the mirror again, there is no noticeable six-pack. This is probably more work than I am prepared to do. I wipe off the sweat with the towel and get dressed quickly.

I grab my phone off the counter and look around. It's still drizzling outside. Hopefully, the two bums who took my ration box are passed out drunk someplace. I flex my arms under the sweatshirt, my muscles whine, and make it known they are wholly unprepared for any sort of self-defense. On top of a pile of clothes by the TV is the CPU I stole from work. I grab the small, black plastic box and stick it in my front pocket, prepared to barter for my life, or at least some potatoes.

My glasses sit on the counter in the kitchen, staring at me blankly. I pause before the door and stare back. They are probably recording me right now. I wonder if that red-haired cop is watching.

If I pull down my pants and perform some penis puppetry, where would the video go? Is it cataloged in a server farm in the desert? Whose job is it to sort through all the amateur pornography looking for criminal activity? Do they offer any benefits and are they looking for help?

I turn and grab the glasses off the counter. I'm just going to the ration station, but they're worth the little bit of extra security they provide. Slipping them over my eyes, they pulse agreeably, purring almost like a cat. I admit, it feels good to have them on. The rioting was much worse before the technology in the glasses became more reliable.

As I exit my building and hit the sidewalk the weather forecast scrolls across the lower half of both lenses. There are frowny rain icons over each day for the rest of the week. They pause to see how our new relationship is progressing, then start rolling out more headlines as I make my way up the street.

"Jones Promises More Taxes on the Rich to Fund Food Science."

"Michaels Tours Aircraft Carrier, Makes Speech Regarding America's Nuclear Capabilities. Promises 'America First' Policy - An End To Humanitarian Aid."

"China on High Alert: Schools Practice Nuclear Air Raid Drills."

I flick on my phone and pull up the WORK app then transfer the search to my glasses. The frames vibrate pleasantly, happy our fight is over. WORK scrolls then pulls up five jobs within a reasonable radius it thinks I would be qualified for. Garbage man is not an option. One of them is as a designer for medical brochures. That could be OK. I blink twice in quick succession, directing WORK to apply on my behalf. The app tells me there are over two-hundred other applicants so far.

I reach the end of the road and take a right, following a line of left-behinders as they shuffle along to nowhere in particular. Everyone is old. They all walk slowly, bundled against the cold and rain, not looking up from where their feet contact the pavement. Some talk to themselves. I keep my head down and do my best to navigate through the crowd without getting too close to any of these people.

I see the ration station in the distance. A line hasn't built up yet.

The old man in front of me stops suddenly and hacks violently into his closed fist. I can't react fast enough and barrel into him as he hunches over, working out whatever is in his lungs. He follows his cough and falls forward, face-first onto the pavement.

Sprawled on the sidewalk, his coughing stops as he rolls over onto his back, moaning. There is a gash on his forehead where he hit the ground. Blood runs down past his bushy eyebrows into his eyes. He blinks twice then squeezes them shut tightly against the gore. His skin is crinkly and weathered and he has a grey beard that hugs most of his neck. Flecks of spittle and other unmentionables are captured in its coarse, winding hairs.

Afraid I am about to be held responsible for his condition, I bend down over him, unsure of what to do. Touching him seems like the worst option. "Are you OK?" my voice squeaks out from my throat.

He moans loudly, not answering.

A similarly weathered woman turns around when she hears the old man. At the sight of blood, she puts her hands to her face dramatically and starts shrieking. "Harry! What did you do to Harry?"

The old woman rushes to Harry's side and bends over to examine his head wound. "You monster! You tried to kill him! You fucking rich-boy monster!" She dabs her finger in his blood and waves it in the air towards me, making wider and wider circles like it's a sparkler on the Fourth of July.

Harry moans loudly, "Oh my head. My head hurts." His eyes are closed tightly shut as blood trickles down his face, pooling under his nose.

The old woman stands up and stabs at my chest with her crimson streaked pointer. "You...you monster. You filthy rich monster...you..."

She's running out of material. I stand up and back away from Harry with my hands up. "Listen lady, it was an accident. I'm really sorry he's hurt, but he just stopped right in front of me and I bumped into him. It was an accident."

"You...you need to make this right, rich-boy." She steps away from Harry and lurches towards me.

Her hair is long and grey, tucked messily under a soiled knit cap. A dress, or something that could have been considered a dress at some point, hangs off her bony frame. Bulky sweatshirts are layered over it. Time and grime have reduced her clothes to nothing more than layers of rags. Her nose is sharp like a spear under her eyes, which I can tell are normally cloudy, but are now clear and focused with anger. Although time and hunger have dulled this skeleton's offensive capabilities, in the face of her rage, I still take two steps backward.

Putting my hands around my shoulders, palms facing towards her, I attempt to plead my case - insanity or perhaps an error in my genetic code. "I'm really sorry. I didn't mean any harm. I was just walking to the ration station."

"You filthy liar! The ration station is closed, rich-boy. There ain't no food. Everyone knows that." She points at me, spitting out the words.

My glasses are listening, a headline splashes across the lens: "Ration Stations Suspend Operations For At Least One Week, National Guard Assures Closures Are Temporary." In my pocket, I feel my phone vibrate as it accepts an account credit for the ration voucher.

Harry sits up, his eyes still closed tightly from the blood spilling out of his head wound. "Veronica!" he calls urgently to the old woman.

She pauses her advance on me for a moment and looks over her shoulder. "Harry, don't try to get up. Just stay where you are."

Others have noticed the commotion. A ring of homeless close in around us, watching. Two of Michaels' campaign street crew, a boy and a girl, move into the crowd. They stand out like shiny pennies.

Ignoring the very real predicament playing out before their lens, my glasses helpfully inform me there is a thunderstorm warning in my area starting at 12 PM today. The two guys from last week quietly join the growing throng. They stand behind Harry as he sits on the ground, clutching his head and moaning. They notice my glasses and pull bandanas over their faces. The short one looks at me and winks evilly.

My glasses tell me to make up for the closing of the ration stations, everyone in my county will be emailed coupons for Go-Bars. And also, to remember the shortage of real food isn't expected to last more than a week.

"Veronica, what's going on here?" the tall one from last week asks.

"Harry are you OK? Did that guy do this to you?" the short one adds, pointing at me. His eyes crease as he frowns theatrically under his hasty disguise.

Harry nods solemnly, wiping at the blood with the bottom of his shirt, exposing his round, hairy stomach. Veronica, sensing a surrogate to carry out her revenge moves away from me, back towards Harry. "This rich-boy-fuck did this to my Harry. He's one of those sick yuppies that beat up the old and the poor for sport." She points her crooked finger at me and then bends down to help Harry dab at his cut.

With some of the blood cleaned off, it doesn't look that bad. It probably doesn't even need stitches. Maybe Harry's just a bleeder.

The short one looks up, serious now. "Yeah, we ran across this guy last week too. Nothing but trouble. What do you want us to do with him?"

A feeling starts in my gut, runs up through my throat, and spills out of my mouth in a dry heave. There seem to be at least a dozen sets of eyes on my sorry carcass, all of them unwashed, all of them cloudy, all of them angry. I was wrong, the glasses haven't provided any extra security.

Desperately, I look for an exit, but there is nowhere to go. I search the area around me for something to weaponize. Nothing. The computer I lifted from work is still in the pockets of my pants. The time to use it as a bartering tool is past. I wrap my fingers around it tightly and pull it out of my pocket. The first one that gets too close to me is going to be bludgeoned.

The tall one notices and points at my hand. "What you got there? Some kind of weapon? Is that what you used to crack old Harry in the skull?" He motions to the crowd. "We aren't going to be bullied by rich, shit-bags like this anymore.

Sitting up in their penthouse condos eating everyone else's rations. Only coming down here with the rest of us to beat up old men so they can share the videos with their yuppie friends in their private chat forums. Did you record it all on your fancy glasses? Do you feel like a big man?" he asks turning towards me.

I feel foolish standing before him, holding this ridiculous computer like it's some sort of weapon. I slide the damn thing back in my pocket and shake my head back and forth, "It was an accident, I bumped into him and he tripped."

Veronica shakes her head violently and glares at me, "Lies! He tripped Harry on purpose. He did it on purpose."

No one here is going to give me the benefit of the doubt. That I exist and that I am in the wrong place at the wrong time is enough of a justification to be a target of their class rage.

I wonder who is watching this ordeal on my glasses. What will they do with the footage when I'm dead? I could use some Big Brothering right now.

The glasses, perhaps sensing my tension, inform me "Michaels Blames Food Shortage on Jones' Policies, Doubles Down on Promises for a Reduction in Aid to Combat World-wide Famine."

My tormentors step past Harry, stalking towards me, grinning. The circle of left-behinders around us tightens like a noose, boxing me in.

"What've you go on ya today?" the taller one asks. "Harry is hurt and you need to make it right. Where's your money, rich boy?"

"Yeah, you're due some reparations." The short one adds.

I don't think he really understands the concept of reparations, but it seems like a bad idea to quibble over the details right now. I feel the violence radiating off them like heat. Their fury ripples through the restless crowd and pings back to the two maniacs standing in front of me, growing stronger with each wave.

I take the computer out of my pocket again, this time without any hope of defending myself. "Look, I'm really sorry. It was an accident. Here take this. Harry can sell it." I hold the CPU out to them on my palm, hopefully.

They're close enough we can touch now. The tall one reaches over and smacks the computer out of my hand. It clatters noisily to the ground.

"That's worthless. What else ya got?"

I shuffle through my pockets and produce my phone.

"Worthless, everyone has one of those pieces of shit."

I take my glasses off and offer them up for sacrifice. The frames buzz in protest.

"What the fuck is Harry supposed to do with those? You want to give him a fuckin' heart attack to go along with the crack in the head?"

I hang the glasses back around my neck and dig my hands into my pockets looking for miracles, finding none.

"That's all I've got guys, I swear. I was laid off from my job. I gave you two of my rations last week. I just eat Go-Bars and sit around. I don't have anything."

What a glorious time to be alive.

The tall one grabs me by the hood on my sweatshirt, bunching it up around my neck. He's holding me like a mother cat carries her kitten. "Put your hands up, rich boy." I decide not to protest and raise my palms to shoulder level.

The short one starts by patting down my pockets. He doesn't find anything interesting. Disappointed, he looks up and shrugs at his friend. I tried to tell them I was worthless.

"Check his jock," the tall one orders.

I squirm at the command and he tightens his grip on my collar. The short one takes a deep breath and grabs the waist of my jeans. I stick my hands in my pockets and hold on for dear life. Harry stops moaning and sits with one hand slowly inspecting the wound, eyes transfixed by the spectacle. Veronica stares at me too, awed by the events she set in motion. I feel the nervous energy of the crowd around us as we silently wrestle for control of my pants. I'm like a gladiator fighting in the Coliseum, except instead of a lion there are two shitheads and instead of swords, shields, axes, and maces, there is only denim and dignity. All things horrible are inevitable and eventually, my grip on my pockets gives way and I'm down to my underwear.

It's clean, no skid-marks, so there's that.

"Nothing," the short one declares.

With a shove, the tall one lets go of my sweatshirt. Panicked, I stumble two steps forward flailing my arms to keep my balance but trip over the pants hanging around my ankles and splatter on the ground.

The short one shrugs and addresses the crowd, "He doesn't have shit." It's meant to have a double meaning and he pauses to accept the chuckles for his verbal acrobatics. I flip over on my back and scramble to pull my pants back up over my underwear. No one in the circle around me makes eye contact, it's too painful. Even for a so-called member of the bourgeoisie, my humiliation is so pathetic it can't be celebrated.

The short one looks around confused. He raises his hands up to the crowd, "Come on. This rich fuck deserved it."

A siren rings out in the distance and it is enough to get people to begin slowly walking away from the circle. Watching me helpless with my pants around my ankles dissipated all their anger. Everyone just feels bad for me.

The tall one realizes they misjudged the level of bloodlust in the crowd and reports back to Veronica, "V, he doesn't have anything."

"Whatever," she replies, waving her hand, dismissing him.

Hoping to salvage some small measure of goodwill, they move away from me and help Harry to his feet. The collar on his shirt is stained red from the blood and his hair is matted. He looks bewildered, his eyes bouncing around searching for some way to make sense of what happened to him. They settle on me and I look away, it's all too much to bear.

"What happened to him?" he asks Veronica, pointing at me on the ground.

"Nothing honey. Come on, let's go get you cleaned up, OK?" she responds, guiding him away by the elbow.

The last stragglers follow them, and I'm left to myself on the cold, damp pavement. I button my pants back up and look around for my dignity. I take out my phone and flip past the lock-screen. My thumb hovers above the phone app. I consider calling the police. I was assaulted.

I watch them meander downtown, bandanas back down around their necks, smoking cigars and talking idly. The short one looks back at me nervously. He sees me holding my phone and elbows the tall one, then they both disappear down a side street.

I look down at the phone again. The urge to call the police passes. No need to pile on myself. My jeans are starting to get wet from the gutter in the pavement. Working without any conscious direction from my brain, my thumb opens the LOVE app. There are three women on this street who are logged in. I wonder how many just witnessed that. Maybe none of them. Maybe all of them.

I never should have left the apartment.

I close the app, hang the glasses back over my nose, and get up off the ground. The large wet spot has been growing on my ass, has made its way towards my crotch.

I look back down the street towards where my apartment is. To get there I would have to pass by at least a dozen people who saw what happened. I need to find a hole to crawl in. I flip my hood up and follow the path of least resistance, keeping my eyes on the ground and steering away from people. When no one is in sight, I run towards nothing, just away from everything.

I feel like crying like a baby. I am alone and pathetic. Perhaps measuring the extra moisture content in my tear ducts or the extra scrunching of my nose, my glasses offer up: "One in Two Americans Are Clinically Depressed, New Study Finds."

Passing through side streets, choosing left or right indiscriminately, I quickly become turned around. The walking helps. It's nice to be lost for a little while.

Hours pass. I feel my glasses pulsing lightly, itching to tell me where I am and where I should go next. I tuck them under my shirt, not ready for my isolation to end just yet. The drizzle continues and the air turns cooler as the sun settles under the horizon. It's not safe to be out here by myself after dark. Part of me is afraid if I let myself settle back into the womb of my apartment I'll never out again.

Between the streets, I get a glimpse of the stacked metal shipping containers that make up the ration station. I take the next right and make my way over. They are abandoned. Someone has spray-painted "CLOSED" in large, crudely drawn letters across the side.

With the meatheads in combat boots who hand out the food nowhere in sight, I feel free to run my hand along the metal sides, dragging my fingers across the spray paint. It's still wet and I smudge the C. Stooping down, I wipe my fingers on the wet tar. The paint mostly slides off. It feels taboo to be this close to the other side of the station. This is where food comes from, this big, dumb, magic box.

A streetlight zips on over my head, struggles for a second, and then goes out again, like a giant bug zapper eating an unlucky insect. I didn't notice how dark it's become. I've been walking for a long time.

Down the street, another set of streetlights flicker on, but the one over my head stays out. There doesn't seem to be anyone else out. The sidewalks are abandoned. Some trash rolls by carried on an empty breeze.

Tonight has the feeling of a zombie apocalypse movie, a poorly executed one. A damp shiver runs up my spine.

I wonder where those two shitheads are hiding now.

A hand grabs my arm at the elbow and pulls me away from the ration station. I jump startled, but the grip remains firmly clutching my elbow, dragging me off down a dark side street.

A small female voice commands, "Don't look around. Just keep walking with your head down."

The voice crawled out from the middle of a black sweatshirt floating over a pair of crunchy jeans and green combat boots. The hood is drawn tightly around her skull with dark sunglasses wrapping across her eyes, making it impossible to see the details of her face. She's shorter than me, the top of her head just barely reaching my shoulder, but somehow, she appears supernaturally strong. I flex my arm against her grip, but it doesn't budge.

I can't remember the last time a female touched me with purpose. Even through a layer of clothing, it maxes out my senses, rendering me useless. I'm nothing more than a man-balloon, being led around by a string, swaying slightly in the breeze.

Her pace quickens as we leave Main Street and move down behind a block of brick buildings. I stumble, struggling to execute the steps of our complicated dance. Her thumb presses painfully into the crook of my elbow as I flounder in her wake. She notices me wincing and loosens her grip, a little.

"Got him. OK, do it," she says into the air.

"What?" I ask. "Do what?"

She looks up at me annoyed and shakes her head "no", then pushes me towards the back of the building. "Cover your ears," she commands.

"What? Why?" I ask.

She shakes her head again in exasperation and pins me up against the wall. My heart beats out of my chest. I stare into the dark center of her hood, my reflection bouncing back off her glasses. My cheeks flush and the first bead of sweat rolls from my hairline into my eyebrow. I look nervous, like a little kid.

She jams her forearm across the top of my collarbone, and we stare at each other, her from behind a curtain and me exposed, nakedly out in the open air. If I wanted to, I think I could break her grip now. I don't want to, so we stay this way, my neurons fully open, bathing in her presence.

"Cover your ears," she repeats calmly.

"Why?"

"Cover them and I'll show you," she offers, easing back off the pressure from her forearm.

I hesitate for a moment, then watch through her sunglasses as my disembodied arms raise and jam pointer fingers into each ear.

"Good. Now, are you going to behave?"

I nod my head. She could have asked me anything and I would have produced the same warm, jelly response. There is a mixture of danger and sex in her touch. It is electric.

With my fingers in my ears, she nods and looks down at the glasses hanging around my neck. "It's suspicious if you destroy them," she says, tucking them gently into my sweatshirt. Then with one hand behind my neck, she guides me to the edge of the building, her hand on my neck is warm and soft. I lose control of my breathing and fall into loose panting. My skin is wet and clammy. I hope she doesn't notice.

We reach the end of the building, and she pushes me back up against the bricks and guides my head to the edge. She places a finger across her lips, then turns her sights down the alley back towards the ration station. She mutters something into her hood again and elbows me in the ribs when she notices I'm still staring at her, panting.

"Watch," she mouths silently.

With fingers still in my ears, I crane my neck around the corner. If anyone was watching from the other side, they would only be able to see my eyes and nose, the world's sweatiest, doughiest Killroy. The ration station sits there, CLOSED graffiti glowing in the dark.

I look back down towards her unsure. Her head stares straight forward, flickering streetlights reflecting off her glasses like spastic fireflies. I follow her lead and stare back down the alley. Her breathing picks up as she begins an almost silent countdown from three.

At "one," the ration station lifts off the ground and twists into a bowtie like a giant has reached down and plucked it off the pavement. It reaches its apex, about fifteen feet off the ground, and pauses, dancing in the air. The sound rushes past, filling the alley with its booming voice, blowing my hair back, staggering me away from my little corner of the building. I trip on the curb and for the second time today, find myself on my ass on the wet pavement. My glasses buzz spastically beneath my shirt, eager to see what's going on, angry about being left out.

She stands resolute in the face of her destructive fury, smiling. A pink lock of hair falls out from underneath her hood, fluttering in the blowback from the explosion.

CHAPTER FOUR

In The Habitat of Bears

Eventually, gravity reclaims superiority, driving the metal carcass of the ration station back into the ground. Little pieces of painted, rusted steel, pavement, and brick rain down on us in our hiding spot behind the building. Smoke fills the street, stinging my eyes, making them water. I look up at her from my seat on the ground.

Through the smoke, her edges appear softer. As the air clears her face comes into focus, it's beaming with the pride of what she has done. The pink strand of hair hangs down across her glasses and dangles in front of her nose. Her septum is pierced across with a pink glass stud and there is a mole on her forehead between her eyebrow and hairline. The rest is still obscured by the dark glasses and hood. Standing over me in the alley, she crackles with life. I'm both afraid to touch her and desperate to. She is the most beautiful thing I have ever seen.

She smiles standing above me and tucks the lock of pink back underneath the hood. "Whoops," she says. Something inside my stomach flips and my skin tingles. This must be what love feels like.

I want her to reach down and pick me up like a baby and carry me away from here. I stare back up at her with my mouth open, trying to think of something to say. Something to make her touch me, but my tongue is like sandpaper against the roof of my mouth, incapable of forming human words or even a sound. I swallow trying to conjure enough moisture to revitalize the dead slug taking up all the room between my teeth. It doesn't do any good.

She sees me struggling to talk and laughs lightly. "We have to destroy to create. Remember that. If we want anything to grow ever again, all of this has to go. They've done nothing but plant weeds and it's choking out all the other life."

She pulls a small notebook from her pocket and reads aloud from an open page. "You cannot make a revolution in white gloves." Her lip cuts up in a snarl and she puts the notebook away again.

I can see myself in the reflection from her glasses, mouth open, gawking awkwardly. This is a lot to process, but it feels important and words fail me. There is a smoldering pile of twisted steel behind us, and she's beautiful and looking at me. I need to say something to keep her here with me forever.

I tuck my legs under my butt on the wet pavement and make it back to my knees. She stares down, not offering any help, watching me struggle to pull myself together. I think she is trying to impress the importance of this on me, the profundity of her protest. It seems like we should move away from here like she should be worried, but a calm exudes from her every pore.

Down the alley, sparks fly as a bulb in one streetlight fizzles and pops. There is a siren in the distance. She peeks around the corner of the building towards the mess she made, then turns and starts walking away from me. Panic rises in my gut; I am failing. I need to do something to keep her from leaving.

I scramble off my ass and whisper, "Wait," at her back.

She turns over her shoulder to look at me but keeps walking down the street. The sirens get louder. My glasses vibrate wildly under my shirt, no doubt eager to tell me all about the dangerous people blowing up government property and just how scary life is.

Her pace quickens as some distance opens between us for the first time in the last ten minutes. It's too much for me to bear, and I break into a sprint down the street following her. She hears my feet slapping the pavement and pivots on her heel as I get close to her. I can't hide the stupid looking smile on my face.

"Don't run, be cool," she hisses between her teeth, annoyed. My face flushes at the scolding. In one motion she turns again and resumes her pace away from the sirens. I match her steps and follow two lengths behind. After ten steps I can see her back straighten and she subtly motions me forward. I moderate my steps and reach her side.

We pass through the labyrinths of streets ringed by three and four-story, mostly old, clapboard apartment buildings, making seemingly random left and right turns. Some of the buildings look abandoned, some show small signs of life; a crack of light showing through a window, a front stoop carefully swept free of leaves. But all of them are worn ragged by countless harsh winters and years of neglect. I've never been down these particular streets before. They are no different than any of the other streets in this town. There is no oasis in this desert of gloom.

There are two men up ahead, sitting on a front step drinking out of paper bags. The pink-haired girl takes her sunglasses off and tucks them into her hair taking care to keep her most revealing characteristic wrapped tightly under the hood. Her eyes are green, and they sparkle under the yellow hue from the streetlights. She looks up at me and sighs then grabs my arm at the elbow, pressing it into her side. My knees buckling for just a second, but I understand the game and will my bones to be solid again. We walk past the two men, arm in arm, like a happy couple. They don't bother looking up.

We take another right at the end of the street. It feels like we're headed towards the green river, but my sense of direction is turned upside down. The sirens are very faint now and continue to fade as we walk.

Out of sight from the men on the stoop, she lets go of my elbow and picks up her pace. My arm still feels warm from where it was joined with her. My brain responds to my heart's commands and releases a fresh round of endorphins, flooding my body. Instead of slapping, my feet now float above the sidewalk.

She looks around. We are alone. My glasses buzz again under my shirt, hungry to see what I see.

"Look, I'm sorry for dragging you into this. It was either pull you aside or watch you get blown inside out with that piece of government garbage. You're welcome, by the way." Her voice is soft and calm, but also strong and confident.

She stares at me waiting for a response. The best I can do is stare back bug-eyed.

She takes a deep breath and continues, "So you just go down that street," she says pointing to her left, "and I'll continue on my way. Forget my face and I'll forget yours and we'll pretend that this never happened, alright?"

I look down the street towards where she is pointing - it looks like a cold lonely apartment, filled with Nacho Go-Bars, Power Flakes, and sadness.

I shake my head, "No. I'm not leaving like that." My voice cracks like a little kid. I clear my throat and try again with more authority, " I want to help."

She rolls her eyes and twirls her finger decisively in the other direction. "Think hard about what you're saying. Trust me, it's a lot easier go back to your life with your phone and your glasses." She emphasizes the last word sharply, almost spitting with contempt.

" I can't. I can't go back." I pause, considering my leverage and if I should play all my cards. She stops walking, digs her heels into the ground, and sets her jaw aggressively.

"I can't forget your face."

"Can't or won't?" she asks, jabbing a finger sharply into my chest.

Her swipe pushes me back a step. I wince but quickly reclaim the ground I lost. For this to work, it seems important to at least make a show of confidence, despite the ongoing liquefaction of my guts.

"I can't. Can we go talk about this somewhere? I saw you blow up that bridge too. I need this. I need something. I won't get in your way. I don't even really know what you're doing but I want to help."

Her face contorts, twisting with anger as she takes in my plea. "So that video they have of me with the bridge, did it come from those?" she asks motioning at my chest. The glasses buzz defensively under my sweatshirt.

"Yeah, maybe...probably," I reply, blushing, "but it wasn't my fault. I had just been laid off and was down by the river watching the sludge when you popped up. There was nothing I could do."

Her face reddens. With a loud snort, she calls up a massive amount of phlegm and spits at my feet. It's a direct hit. The wad of her goo finds a home on the toe of my left sneaker.

"Listen, you fuck, there is a big misunderstanding going on here," she steps forward, chest to chest I can feel her breath, hot with rage, against my throat, "I saved your stupid ass this one time, but that doesn't mean I give two shits about what happens to you."

A lump made entirely out of tears and self-pity starts in my stomach and travels up the pipes inside me. It lodges itself in my throat. I take a hiccup breath and one step back from the pink-maned, fire breathing dragon camping in my personal space. Sensing my weakness, she closes the gap and steps towards my chest again, unwilling to let me off the hook I'm dangling from.

This feels like a big moment in my life. Vaguely, some-where in the background of my mind, a teacher tells me the best way to avoid being bullied is with direct confrontation. That seems like bullshit, designed to embolden a different species of human. A tear slips past my frayed nerves and rolls down the inside of my nose. I quickly dig at it with my middle finger and turn away. Her face softens involuntarily, either from compassion or revulsion. I can't tell.

"I can't forget."

She backs away from me and looks towards the ration station. The sirens echo off the walls of our brick cocoon. Footsteps ring out from some alleyway.

"We need to keep moving," she concedes bitterly, nodding in the direction of the footsteps.

I nod, cutting off another drip with my finger before it can begin its voyage down my face, and she jogs off towards the sludge river. I follow behind her, walking with long strides, doing my best to be inconspicuous, but if anyone is watching, we couldn't look more suspicious. She winds us down two alleys and the footsteps and sirens fade away. The brick opens into violent green, and we're back at the river where I saw her for the first time. It's fully dark now, clouds from the rain earlier in the day cover up the moon. The streetlights don't penetrate the fog by the river's banks. She puts more distance between us, and I have to squint to make out her shape amongst the dilapidated clapboard houses that line the river. She trots across a porch, lightly stepping past the rotted floorboards like a ghost, like she's trying to ditch me.

I pick up the pace, churning my legs into a sprint, and follow her past the last house on the block into a wooded lot with a public trail winding through it. Under the canopy of pine trees and half-bald maples, the darkness is complete. I rocket down the path as fast as I can, desperate to keep her close. The floor is slick with fallen leaves, twisted roots pierce through the dirt, eager to break an ankle or a foot.

Her shape bobs up and down in the dark about twenty yards in front of me, navigating the dangerous terrain with an ease born of familiarity. I stumble and claw my way through the path, desperately struggling to keep her in my sight. I don't even know her name. I used my knowledge as leverage, but the truth is, if she disappeared into the black ether right now, I would not know how to see her again.

"Hey, wait for me!" I yell into the darkness, scrambling across particularly cumbersome, unseen roots. Her shape is completely lost to me now. The combination of physical activity and fear turns my organs into a raging inferno. Sweat is dripping out of all my pores.

She's gone. I lost her. I stop my mad dash and listen into the darkness. There are no sounds, no twig snapping, no leaf scrunching, only my ragged, chunky breathing disturbs the silence. My eyes adjust to the blackness and it's clear that at some point I lost the path. I've walked this route a few times during lunch breaks at Delicious Designs, but it's unrecognizable in the dark. Surrounded by tall pines I can't tell which way I came and which way I'm going.

A new fear sets into my heart, the fear not just of losing her, but of being lost myself. There is an outcropping of rocks nestled amongst the pines. I go over and take a seat, wrapping my arms around my body, trying to beat back the chill from my cooling sweat. The darkness envelops me like a cold blanket. I'm probably going to have to spend the night out here. Though it's not worse than my shitty apartment.

My glasses buzz to remind me they are the portal to all knowledge that has been accumulated by humanity and if only I would put them on again and let them take a look around they could help me find my way out of this thicket. It's tempting, but I would rather spend the night out here than give in and let them lead me back home.

Suddenly the silence is shattered, and the forest is alive with an unseen limb, snapping, and snarling in fury. I must have interrupted a bear or something, maybe I'm near a cave. I sit motionless on my rocky perch trying to avoid whatever large animal is rampaging through the thicket.

A large shape emerges before me in the dark blocking out the remaining reflection of the moon. It is huge and advances, seeing me better than I can see it. I don't know what to do, so I do what comes most naturally, nothing. Strong hands reach out to me, grasping my body with their violence. Sitting stone-faced, I accept my fate as the pitch-black crashes down around me.

CHAPTER FIVE

I've Seen
This on the Internet

My father died, after contracting a penicillin-resistant infection when I was thirteen. The doctors said he got it swimming during a trip to the cottage that we called, 'the Coop,' that my grandparents had built on Fortune's Rocks beach. He cut his foot on a piece of glass and some "super-bug" got into his blood.

We brought him to the hospital the next day when his temperature spiked and then waited for three days before agreeing to saw his foot off. By then the infection had spread up his leg, into his heart and had been pumped through the rest of his arteries. Two weeks after taking his foot, the doctors sent him home in a wheelchair with a bandaged stump and a prescription for morphine. He insisted on us taking him back to the Coop.

We had a hospital bed set up in the living room and for the first week, he entertained a never-ending stream of brothers, sisters, aunts, uncles, and cousins coming through to visit him one last time. He gritted through the pain, smiling when he could, telling stories of a childhood with summers spent at the cottage, swimming, lobstering, and stealing beers from drunk adults during the Fourth of July celebrations, only giving in to tears after whichever visitor sitting by his bedside succumbed to them first.

After that week, the pain became too much. The morphine drip would dry up early in the morning and his howls would wake the whole house. My mom, with the help of a visiting nurse, upped the dosage and set her alarm to swap in a new bag before the pain took hold. After that, he mostly slept. People still dropped by to hold his hand and feed him ice chips, but he was already gone. His body finally gave out three weeks later.

During my time at Delicious Design, I would think about him while sitting in my climate-controlled box, trying to decide: three prongs or four - a twenty-five-degree curve on the handle or twenty-two and a half? When I was little, he had me convinced I was going to be a professional baseball player. He would carry me around on his shoulders and makeup stories about my pitching for the Red Sox.

I was young and naive enough to adopt his dreams as my own. We would play catch in the backyard – a Rockwellian scene, no doubt. My dad would shout, "good boy" whenever I snapped off a fastball with enough force to hit the webbing in his glove and make it pop.

He was a short man with a small, springy gait that would rock me to sleep on his shoulders as I bounced up and down with my face resting on his scalp. I used to roll my fingers through his soft brown hair, grab a lock and rub it compulsively against my upper lip, until I fell asleep, dreaming of throwing ninety miles-an-hour pitches and hitting sky-scraping home runs. When I woke his hair would be glued to the corners of my mouth by the spittle that had leaked out while I drooled. There were lots of scary, mysterious things about life, but nothing could get at me while I traveled on his shoulders. There it was safe to have dreams.

I've never slept better than I did on his shoulders when I was five.

The sensation is familiar, a weightless bounce that starts in my core and reverberates through my spine into my skull, pleasantly tickling my brain. It makes me giggle and I become aware that I'm asleep. I try to hold onto the illusion of the memories, to curl back up inside the past, but my brain won't indulge my frivolity, choosing instead to bring my systems back online. Disappointed, I open my eyes, transporting upside-down images of a leaf-strewn ground interspersed with gleaming black boots, to my brain.

Awake now, I find my jaw hanging agape, clicking my teeth together as my body bobs up and down. I close it with a snap and taste steely blood. It takes a moment to process exactly what is happening to me, draped upside-down across some unusually large man's shoulders, being carried off in some unknown direction. Processing this in real-time, my brain floods my capillaries with panicked adrenaline, stiffening my helpless body. I make a fist and jab it weakly into my transport's lower back, something like a squeal makes its way across my lips.

"Motherfucker, you try 'n hit me again and I promise you, it'll be the last damn thing your dumb-ass ever does." The voice booms down over my shoulder as a powerful arm tightens its vise across my waist.

Ignoring the warning and all good sense, adrenaline forces a series of bad decisions on my body sending my hands first groping upwards then full of thick hair. Reflexively, I pull hard on this newfound lever and anxiously await whatever wonders it will unleash.

It works! The comforting sensation of weightlessness returns as my shepherd exits me off his shoulder, helicoptering my body through the night air, before finally landing on the trail with a hard thump.

A large root system catches me under my armpit, knocking the wind from my lungs. I cough and wince as more blood trickles from my mouth and down my chin. Clutched sweaty in my palm is a dreadlock, crisscrossed with black and grey hair. Its owner glares down at me angrily. He touches his fingers to a spot on the back of his head that formerly housed the hair in my hand and brings them back bloody, waving his fingers in front of my face. That makes me responsible for two bloodlettings in one day. Truly now I am engaged in the full experience of humanity.

"What the fuck did I just tell you? You fucked up now. Big time." The man steps towards me growling, eyes glowing with naked hatred.

I scramble backward along the piles of dead leaves and fallen pine needles. He has an unconquerable advantage and closes the gap effortlessly, looming over me, curling his fingers into enormous fists.

"Cap! Don't! Let it go, OK?" The girl with the pink hair emerges from behind him and places a hand calmly on his arm.

"Fuck that. I warned this little motherfucker and he didn't listen."

"I know, he panicked. We don't have time for this, we have to get back. Please, just let it go this time. You know how they can be at first."

I watch dumbly as they negotiate the terms of my continued existence.

She squeezes his arm and repositions herself between us, looking up at him. "Please, let it go. Please."

He tries to resist, but his body language betrays him, slumping his shoulders and deflating his chest. He opens his mouth to argue with her but then gives up and sighs.

"Next time, motherfucker. Next time, I promise you. And give me back my fucking hair." Bending down, he snatches the orphaned dread out of my sweaty clutch. I let it go easily, happy for the trade. He holds it up to eye level, grunts, and stuffs it into a pocket.

"He's your problem now, Sam," he says turning his back. "You want him alive then you drag his dumb ass around."

Sam exhales and extends her hand to me. I take it and get up off the ground. My mouth hurts.

"You decided to follow me, huh?" she says sighing.

Smearing the back of my hand across my mouth I wipe the blood on my pants.

"What happened?"

"Cap got the jump on you in the woods..."

"Yeah, motherfucker, and I should have finished the job," Cap interjects, taking the hair back out of his pocket and waving it in my direction. "Should have let that motherfucker get blown-the-fuck-up with those metal boxes," he adds, turning his attention back to Sam.

"OK, fine, but we can sort this out later, we need to keep moving," Sam says, ushering us away from the standoff with both hands.

"You picked quite a time to get all bleeding heart and shit," Cap adds out of the corner of his mouth, but the argument is over. "I was tired of carrying your doughy ass anyway. And Sam's right, get your ass moving."

Satisfied Sam starts down the trail waving for me to follow. My hesitation is met with a strong shove from behind, snapping my neck back.

"Move," Cap booms.

I don't hesitate again, skipping forward two steps to catch up to Sam's heels. We're in a different part of the town-forest than I have ever been in. There is no river smell where we are and we're heading downhill.

I've never been knocked out before but judging from the distance we've traveled; I must have been gone for some time. I probably have a concussion. I think that means I could die if I fall asleep, which might be easier than whatever Cap has in mind for me.

We reach the bottom of the hill and the moon is back out, shining down through the bare branches. It's clear Sam is not following any established path but even in the bad light, she steps with the surety of a mountain goat, agile and confident in her movements.

Struggling to keep pace, with Cap threatening at my back, I stumble blindly after her. She takes her hood down, apparently now comfortable with our familiarity. Her hot pink hair tumbles out, reaching more than halfway down her back. It billows in her wake as she scales obstacles in her path.

I turn over my shoulder and take a better look at Cap. He's wearing dark green coveralls tucked into a pair of black military boots. A large pack is strapped sideways across one massive shoulder. His skin is as dark as the forest around us, features indistinguishable under the cover of night. A toothpick juts out from the corner of his mouth, held in place comfortably as if a part of him. Cap sneers when he sees me looking back, his teeth glowing menacingly.

"Turn the fuck around, stupid. Worry about your own damn self," he pants.

The pack he's wearing looks heavy, he looks less like a gazelle in this setting and more like a rhinoceros. I could probably slip away from them right now. Wait it out until daylight and be done with this madness.

They could be taking me anywhere, someplace deep in the woods where they can take their sweet time dismembering me in private, scattering my pieces for the animals to find. But this is what I asked for, what I begged for back in town, what I refused to take 'no' as an answer for. This is something different, for once, and it feels good to take a risk.

In front of me, Sam starts heading up another hill. She climbs it at a sprint that seems almost superhuman. I have to bend over and use my hands to steady my feet against a slippery avalanche of leafy debris.

"Yo, Sam, slow-the-fuck-up. Jesus Christ, nobody's chasing us. Shit." Cap is having an even harder time with the climb than I am. She reaches the top of the hill and stops, watching as we struggle.

We make it to the top and Cap says, "Next time, Imma make you carry your own damn pack."

She laughs and prods him playfully in his large midsection. "You need the exercise, big boy. Did you see that thing explode? The setup worked perfectly. We must have blown it twenty feet up into the air."

"Yeah, I saw it," Cap replies, smiling subtly. "Don't know why you're surprised. All the shit I make works, every time."

I'm the world's most obvious fly on a wall.

Cap frowns and motions towards me, "So what are we gonna do with this motherfucker?"

I'm the biggest turd in the world's punch bowl.

Sam shrugs. "You know how it is. I couldn't just leave him there to get blown to hell too. And then he wouldn't stop following me and he saw my face... I didn't see any other option. It was either bring him with or wait for the police to catch up to us." Her voice rises dramatically.

Cap shifts the toothpick back and forth from one corner of his mouth to another, thinking. He looks me up and down like a piece of luggage, starting at my toes and ending at the top of my skull, a chill passes through me.

" What's your fucking deal, huh?" he asks with a nod.

This is the most difficult question that has ever been put to me. What is my deal? I look towards Sam for some help, but she stands next to Cap with her hands on her hips, waiting for whatever shitty answer I can manage.

I suck some spit across my tongue, hoping hydration can will it back to life. My brain is blank, but standing silently, staring at them stupidly isn't going to cut it in this situation. There must be a semblance of a survival instinct, buried deep inside for occasions like this, some internal steel to keep me from being churned into pink mush by the gears of life. I open my mouth to respond and my tongue peels off the roof of my mouth, slapping against my teeth like a dead fish, producing only a scared sounding gurgle.

"What the fuck did he just say?" Cap demands of Sam, pointing at me with one enormous finger.

Sam shrugs, as confused as I am, but unwilling to coach me into something better.

"Speak up, white boy. Say something for yourself." Cap glares at me fiercely, his chest puffed out in a peacocking show of strength. "You dumb, stupid, mute, or what?"

We're out in the wild, stripped out of the protective cocoon that has allowed me to walk through life virtually unscathed. We're animals now, naked, capable of raw, unfettered, and unrepentant violence - time to act accordingly.

I try again, opening my mouth, unsure of what exactly will come out.

"I don't have a deal. There is no deal." The words pass my lips but are barely above a whisper.

"Stop mumbling and talk like a man. Make me feel it. Make me feel something, or your family will never find your rotten carcass." Cap pounds one meaty hand against his chest menacingly.

"I don't have any FUCKING DEAL, OK? My name is Jake. I live here. I do bullshit to get paid. I sit around wasting time until it's time to either shit or eat. I don't have a deal." Cap's shoulders fall backward, apparently unprepared for me to follow his command. I press forward riding the wave before it's lost.

"I saw what you guys did to that bridge and to the ration station. I saw them explode and it is the first meaningful thing I have seen in my life. There is nothing there for me and I want to watch it all burn."

All of that seems true to me. It feels like a flame has been lit inside me, partly Sam, partly something else more urgent and destructive. My glasses buzz meekly against my chest, apparently worried by my newly formed convictions.

Sam allows a small smile to part her lips. She looks beautiful. I think about what it would be like to kiss her, to press against her and hold her tight, to have her hold me back. She's the real reason I'm here, in the middle of the woods, on a cold night with only sociopaths for company.

Cap recovers quickly from the initial shock of the appearance of my backbone. "Man, you are full of shit," he spits on the ground at his feet, passing the toothpick back and forth with his teeth. I hold his eye contact. It's a stand-off.

"This is fucking stupid," he says at last, breaking the tension. "If he's going to be here, then he's your problem, but if he gets in my way, I don't care what anyone says, I'm putting him in the ground."

I'm getting used to being discussed like I'm not there.

"Did you mean it?" Sam asks.

"Mean what?"

"That you want to watch it burn?"

I consider the question along with the risks inherent when one opens their mouth and lets thoughts out for a walk. Sam and Cap stand together watching me. If I take too much time, whatever I say will seem like a lie. I nod.

Sam moves closer to me, leaving Cap's side. "You should leave now, but if you want to stay, you're going to have to make a decision. It has to be your decision and you're going to have to want it. Understand?"

I don't understand but again I use my skull to signal the universal gesture for "yes."

"Good. Not today, but sometime soon, I'm going to ask you a question and you are going to have to decide and there won't be any going back after." She looks at me with a furrowed brow waiting for a real answer.

"Ok," I croak hoarsely. "Ok."

Apparently satisfied, Cap turns and moves off deeper into the woods. It's just Sam and me, standing together in the cold night. Hot breath billows out of our mouths in white clouds, commingling in the space between us, then disappears. Sam's green eyes sparkle out at me, glowing in the dark. Adrenaline pumps through my veins, making it hard not to pant, even in the cold. I reassert control over my internal systems and wait for her to decide the fate of things. There is no point in over-extending and exposing myself any further than I already have.

Sam takes a deep breath, tasting the air before letting it leak out of her nose in white puffs. It looks like she's smoking.

"Well, let's get on with it then. Follow me." She turns on her heel and follows Cap off into the blackness. I hesitate for a second then jog after her neon hair as it floats through the trees. As we push through the underbrush, prickers rip at my pants.

Off any discernible path, I follow her blindly, choosing my steps as carefully as her pace will allow. In the distance, I see the small flicker of a campfire, struggling to life. That must be where Cap lumbered off to.

We burst through the dense brush and onto a cleared pad ringed by birch trees. Water trickles from a nearby stream. Two camouflage tents circle an old, one-room shack, about the size of three outhouses. In the middle, Cap tends a small fire, feeding twigs into the flames as it crackles and pops. The toothpick has been relocated to the spot behind his ear, replaced by a small, sweet-smelling cigar. He doesn't look up as we enter the camp.

"We're low on firewood."

Sam walks right by him into the shack. She comes out holding a plastic water jug, takes a deep drink, and looks around.

"I thought you were gonna get more firewood this after-noon, before we left for town," Cap says with his palms facing up in front of his chest.

"Sorry, I forgot. Too much excitement, I guess," Sam explains with a shrug, taking another deep pull from the water jug.

"Well, we don't have enough to last the night, and I don't want to burn up all the batteries in the flashlight looking for more."

"Sorry," Sam replies with a smile. "Don't be all grouchy, today was great. Everything was perfect."

"I know it was perfect," he says shooting me a look to make it clear I am not included in his definition of "perfect." "I told you, all I fucking do is *perfect*. But now we don't have any firewood, and my ass is gonna be cold all night. I fucking hate being cold." Cap places a log on the fire and stands up. "Plus, now we got this dumb motherfucker all up in our camp. Let's review, all the shit I did today; building bombs, making clean get-aways, all my shit was perfect, and all the shit you did today; forgetting firewood, selling us out, was fucked up."

Sam tries to hold the laugh back, but it snorts through her nose. "Come on Cap, I'm sorry. I'll make it up to you. Tomorrow, I get two days' worth of firewood and I'll boil the water. Fair?"

"Yeah, whatever," Cap replies sitting back down and taking a long drag from his skinny cigar.

Turning to me, Sam says, "You'll get used to Cap, he isn't as bad as he sounds."

"Where the fuck is he supposed to sleep? In your tent?" Cap asks flames reflecting across his eyes.

Sam joins him by the fire, takes off her boots, and stretches her toes out towards the warmth. "It's not like that," she says, laughing at his ridiculousness. "He can sleep in the shack. We have that extra sleeping bag."

Flames lick the new log Cap placed on top of the brush then greedily spread across it. Cold, I move closer to the pair and sit down on the other side of the pit from Cap. Sam nods at me approvingly, and I lean in closer, rubbing my hands at the edge of the heat.

Silence takes over, as the three of us watch the fire dance along the wood, Cap smoking, and brooding.

"Is that water safe?" I ask, nodding towards the little brook. It's been a while since I've seen water that wasn't choked out by algae.

"It comes down from the mountains, swelling in the spring after the thaw. It might be OK, but we boil it, just in case. Are you thirsty?" Sam asks, holding out the water jug towards me.

I nod, take the container, and gulp from it. It's been a long day.

"Do you want something to eat?" Sam asks. "We have saved up some provisions in the shack."

Cap rolls his eyes in annoyance, and shakes his head, taking a long drag from his cigar. He mutters, "Didn't even come with food. Unbelievable," under his breath.

Sam smiles at me and nods towards the shack reassuringly. "There is a stack of Go-Bars on the shelf to the left as you walk in. Grab me one too, OK?"

I shudder at the prospect of another one of those sawdust squares but do my best to hide it from Sam. I'm thankful for even the smallest kernel of her kindness.

A flashlight hangs from a screw on the outside wall of the shack. I pick it up and cross the threshold. There is no door. Inside the uninsulated walls are ringed with shelving. A seemingly random collection of objects and knickknacks are jammed onto every flat surface, occupying almost every square inch of space. It's dizzying to look at. Up to my left are three boxes of bars. I pull two out and head out of the shack, hanging the light back on the wall.

"Thanks," Sam says, as I hand her one.

Cap stares into the fire, enjoying his smoke, ignoring me.

I open my bar and make a show of being grateful for the food. "So, what are you guys doing, exactly?" I ask.

Cap snorts at the question, shaking his head.

Sam nibbles at her bar and considers my question. Reaching into a pocket hidden in her sweatshirt, her hands return holding the small, weathered notebook.

"Well, we're making a point. We're waking people up to reality. They're hiding the ball from everyone, distracting them with their shiny new bits of technology, from the facts of life. The sheep have been turned into robots; herding replaced by programming."

Sam hits her open palm with her fist for emphasis then starts flipping through the notebook, stopping on a page with her thumb. "The first duty of a man, or a woman, is to think for themselves. Jose Marti wrote that. I added the part about a woman." She closes the book, satisfied, and puts it back into the folds of her clothes.

I've seen videos of people like this on the internet.

"We blow up pieces of their infrastructure, if for no other reason than to make people look up for at least a second, and maybe get a chance to see what they have become. Oh, we have bigger targets in mind. Bigger plans than what we've done so far. This is only the warm-ups."

Sam's chest swells with importance as she describes their mission. She looks so proud and sure of herself. I couldn't love her more. When she finishes, Cap chortles and leans back away from the fire.

"You asking me too?" he asks.

I hesitate, gulp but then nod.

"I do it because of all that shit Sam said, but also because fuck them and fuck you. Understand? Fuck *it* all."

He emphasizes the "it," letting the word roll off his tongue, then holding onto the T. He smiles and takes another drag from the cigar.

I turn back to Sam, "And you guys just live out here and run into town on these missions..."

Cap laughs and repeats my last word to himself quietly, looking up as a deposit of sap in the firewood boils then pops, sending sparks flying into the air above our heads.

"We're camping," Sam explains with a wry grin. "We decide on a target. Cap wires up the explosives and gives them to me. I go into town and place them, then we come back here."

"Yeah, that's right. And Sam gets to do all the blowin' up, because here in this stupid, cold-ass state of yours, even a chick with pink hair stands out less than a tall, fine, brother, like myself."

"Cap and I met in Florida and have been picking our way up the east coast, trying to stay ahead of whatever attention we attract."

"Why are we telling him all this shit anyway?" Cap addresses the question to Sam with one large index finger pointing at me.

"He seems harmless. You're harmless, right?" Sam asks me with a wink. "He wants to watch it burn too." She laughs at this last part.

My stomach flips into a knot, releasing butterflies throughout my body, and I shake my head, eager to convince Cap I am harmless and capable of blowing up the world and should stay.

"Harmless my ass. Where are the rest of those shitty, fucking bars?" Cap gets up and heads into the shack, moving things around, noisily.

"He's not so bad," Sam says again. "But you really shouldn't have followed me back from the ration station. We'll talk about the rest of it tomorrow."

She gets up and goes over to her tent, returning with a puffy camouflage sleeping bag.

"Here," she says dropping it into my lap. "I have an extra. It gets cold out here at night."

Cap comes out of the shack, chewing loudly with a box of Go-Bars under one giant arm. "I'm going to bed," he says without looking at either of us.

Sam watches him unzip his tent, plop down inside, and zip it back up without another word. "I'm going to bed too," she says with a smile, turning back to me. "Just let the fire die out. You should be fine with that sleeping bag in the shack. Goodnight."

"Goodnight," I repeat back to her, as she stands up and moves into her tent on the other side of the fire, away from Cap.

The only sound in the forest around me is the hiss and fizz as the fire works its way through the wet wood. I'm alone, a million miles away from home. Perhaps sensing my isolation, my glasses buzz underneath my shirt. I'd forgotten about them. Even out here alone, the buzzing has a Pavlovian effect on my brain. Resisting the urge to put them on and plug back in is enough to make my skin crawl. I look around the camp into the dark.

So, this is it. A shiver runs through me. I wrap the sleeping bag around my shoulders and inhale deeply. It smells like Sam.

The fire dies down slowly as the night pushes back, reclaiming the space it had loaned to the flames, filling in the gaps around me with blackness.

CHAPTER SIX

Like Wiped Away Puke

The sun rose quickly over the makeshift camp, sending light streaming through the holes in the old barn boards of the shack. It's still cold out, and I huddle inside the sleeping bag, letting the enormity of the decisions I've made during the last twenty-four hours wash over me. I can't stop the smile from creeping across my face.

Underneath the covers, I take inventory of myself. My jeans, shoes, and sweatshirt are all crusted with filth and blood, unseemly but functional. Across my chest, underneath the layers of dirty clothes, the glasses remain unscathed, carving out a familiar groove in my flesh. I run my hands along my pockets, my wallet and phone are gone, probably lost when Cap carried me around like a sack of potatoes.

If someone were to come across them in the woods, they would probably think I was taken by a mountain lion or a bear or a moose with rabies. No one would be able to guess my true fate. The smile on my lips deepens as I flip over on my back. It's hard not to be proud of myself. I feel strong, dangerous. I slept the night in the woods, like a fugitive or a soldier.

I pull my hands out of the sleeping bag and raise them over my face, curling the fingers into fists. Running my knuckles back and forth over my lips, they feel hard and lumpy, capable of inflicting great harm in the most just of circumstances. I resolve that if I ever see those two bums who pantsed me in the street, I'll knock their teeth straight down their scuzzy throats.

The fantasy is intoxicating. I let the scene play out in my mind; me walking down the middle of the road, them hassling some young woman, maybe Sam. They're grinning like coyotes as I approach, but their expressions change as I get closer. They can see I've hardened since our last encounter and they're afraid. Dropping their assault on Sam, they prepare to defend themselves, but it's too late. I'm on them, hitting the tall one with a straight left across the bridge of his nose. He yelps and falls to the ground. I pivot slightly to the left and hit the small one with an uppercut. His jaw clicks as his teeth come together clipping off the end of his tongue. His scream turns into a gurgle as the tip falls to the pavement. I follow the uppercut with another straight left to his eye socket, crushing it. The two thugs writhe in pain on the ground in front of me. I step on the dismembered tongue, squishing it under my sneaker like a big fat slug.

"What the fuck are you smiling about?" Cap booms from the door of my little shelter, startling me into lucidity. The triumph of my violence shatters as quickly as I conjured it.

"Man, get the fuck up, I'm hungry." Cap pushes me aside easily with one foot, sliding the sleeping bag across the floor with me in it. Then he walks past and starts rummaging through the shelves. Debris flies as he knocks anything in his way onto the floor, muttering louder and louder as his search for something edible becomes more futile.

"Sam!" Cap bellows, turning his back and stretching his neck out of the shack. "Where is the rest of the food? I can't eat any more of these tasteless shit-bars."

There is no response.

"Sam!" Cap snaps as he stomps off towards the fire pit.

I peek my head out of the shelter and take a look. The camp is a mess. Go-Bar wrappers and water jugs are strewn across the ground.

I don't see Sam anywhere. Cap trudges around the fire pit, sparing no corner in his search for something edible. I spot Sam on the hill above us, early morning light streams around her petite frame. Gone are the baggy sweatshirt, cargo pants, and boots. Seemingly impervious to the cold, she's dressed only in a sports bra and shorts, limbs orchestrating a beautifully coordinated series of movements, her breath going in and out in tight rhythmic puffs.

The plot of my life has shifted considerably in the past twenty-four hours. I don't have the depth of experience to put true words to what I am seeing. If I had to guess, it's tai chi or something. Whatever it is, it's beautiful and mesmerizing, but a sense of uneasiness permeates the moment for me. The scene is so perfect, it looks orchestrated like it was placed here for me to wake up to and wonder in dumb amazement.

Sam sees me watching and smiles, calmly pushing air nowhere with one open palm. Suddenly, I don't care if this show is for my benefit or completely genuine. She could tell me to drink from the river, and I would fall forward on my knees with a smile and shovel the green gunk into my jaws. Butterflies break out and beat their wings against my stomach lining. An erection pokes against the crotch of my pants. I wrap the sleeping bag tighter around me and try not to think about beautiful, wild things wearing sports bras.

Cap spots her up on the bluff. "More of that hippy bullshit. You get a good look?" he growls at me.

"Yo Sam," he yells in her direction. "Where is the rest of the real food?"

"There are two apples in the pack, inside my tent," she responds calmly without breaking the stride in her movements.

Cap shakes his head, trudges over to her tent, and enters brusquely without removing his boots. Somehow his skepticism feels like validation like I've discovered a secret. It makes me feel better about allowing myself to continue falling headlong into the dream that is her. Cap emerges holding both apples and seats himself by the remains of last night's fire, carving up the fruit into pieces with a pocketknife and his gigantic thumb. His rage is temporarily satiated by the presence of real food, still, I avoid eye contact.

I am far out of my depth. Underneath my sweatshirt, the glasses buzz aggressively. Desperate for a distraction to calm the pulsing, urgency awakening beneath me, I succumb and lift the glasses onto my nose. It's a calculated risk, that no one is looking for me yet and this will just be a small piece in a sea of data. I make sure to keep the glasses trained away from Cap, Sam, and any other potentially identifying details. They purr reveling in their victory, pleased their obedient dog has returned.

The news scroll begins immediately: "Ration Station Closed Indefinitely, Officials Blame Local Terrorists For Lack Of Fresh Food."

I blink the story away to see what else there is: "China and Russia Finalizing Treaty, Threaten Immediate Retaliation If Michaels Wins Election."

It works. Capillaries reopen inside me and begin the process of diverting blood back to their normal functions. In an overabundance of caution, I blink through to the next story: "Experts Deny Overpopulation Myth, Noting Significant Decrease in Life Expectancy. Michaels Decries Pseudo-Science, Calls Catastrophic Famine a 'Problem Solver'." I feel digitally neutered.

Able to stand again, I tuck the glasses back into their hiding spot, gently roll up the sleeping bag and make my way out of the little shack, with it tucked under my arm. Sam is back down from her spot on the hill. I hand her the sleeping bag and she disappears into her tent, remerging dressed more appropriately for the morning chill. I wait for her to return and then we both join Cap around the pit where he has started a small fire.

"Y'all are stuck eating those fucking bars," Cap says around bites of the second apple. "I'm not dealing with that bullshit anymore."

Sam passes me a Go-Bar from out of the box and shares her jug of water. The combination passes through my esophagus and hits my stomach like a brick - take that digestive enzymes!

We all sit and chew, staring into the growing fire. I feel like a kid sitting outside the principal's office, waiting to find out if they are going to call my parents or not.

Eventually, Sam breaks the silence, "So are you ready to head back to town today?" She looks at me earnestly with her big eyes, aware of the mounting control she is building over me.

I choose to ignore the question, "What do you guys have planned next?"

"Not carrying your deadweight-ass around, that's for sure," Cap replies, sending tiny apple pellets flying into the fire.

Ignorance has always been my best defense.

Sam takes my hand between hers and says, "We...I, can lead you back to the path after you finish and you can get back to your life. It's probably the best thing for everyone, especially you." Her touch sends my neurons spasming out of control, it's almost too much to handle. A bundle of nerves in the base of my feet begin vibrating, trying desperately to simulate what it's like to walk on a cloud.

I think I'm going to pass out.

Sam notices and starts rubbing the top of my hand with her thumbs. This is unfair.

Cap watches the dance going on between us, shakes his head, and resumes staring into the fire.

I curl my toes, pressing the soles of my feet back into the earth and do my best to combat her. "I don't have anything to go back to. I want to stay here with you."

"Honey..." Sam starts. This is like fishing for minnows with an atom bomb.

"I've seen your face, where you camp," I say meekly, my scrambled brain only capable of repeating threats that have worked in the past.

"Yeah, you have. And if you tell anybody, I'll find you and kill you," Cap says matter-of-factly, through a mouthful of apple.

"But that won't be necessary," Sam says soothingly. "Right, Jake?"

Gooseflesh breaks out across my arms at the sound of hearing her say my name. I wish my infatuation wasn't so clearly on display for Cap to see. Holding any leverage in this situation is all but impossible. The physical contact is almost too much to resist, I stand up and move two steps away from Sam, hoping a little distance is enough to sever the puppet strings she has on me. I make sure not to venture too close to Cap.

"Listen, I can be helpful with what you guys have going on here. I know I can. I grew up here. I know my way around. I know how to get anything you need. I want to help you. Let me do it." Even to my ears, my voice sounds whiny, pleading like a little kid negotiating their bedtime.

Cap snickers as Sam rolls her eyes.

Raising my voice and tapping my chest, I steel myself to move forward, making a play at seeming undeterred, "I could put these things back on right now and blow this whole little shin-dig up." My voice cracks unconvincingly when I say shin-dig.

Cap pauses, processing my words then laughs, unconvinced by my threat, "Man, fine whatever. Stick the fuck around. See what happens to you."

Sam's face twists into a smirk at Cap's concession. The longer I stay within her reach, the better. The humiliation yesterday with Harry and the mob has started to fade. This is what victory tastes like, morning breath and rice flour.

"What do we do now?" I ask, faking a cheeriness into my voice, hoping I'm part of the team now.

"*We* don't do shit. What *you* do is to go get *me* some food, some real fucking food. I can't sit out here in the woods eating this chalk dust anymore." Cap fires one of the apple cores into the fire. Sparks float up like lightning bugs then fizzle out.

"You want to be around here. Job number one for you is to provide something other than pasty insecurity. You do that and I'll take your continued presence here on a day-to-day basis. Got it?"

That is the most reasonable offer Cap has ever extended to me during our brief relationship.

He looks towards Sam. "Might as well bring his ass down to that farm and pick up some groceries."

"I don't think we should go back there," Sam warns. "It didn't go so well the first time."

Cap grins widely. "No, it didn't. But I'm not eating any more of this bullshit and you don't have any other options."

"You aren't going to come with us, are you?" Sam asks.

"Fuck, no. I'm done fucking around with the crazy white people around here. Too many guns. You take him with you, stand behind him like a human shield or some shit. Can't leave him here anyway. Dumbass is likely to do something stupid if left on his own." He mutters the last sentence to himself and gets up from his stump.

"I'm going to go take a dump in the woods, get this concrete shit out of my stomach before it hardens, and kills me. Don't be here when I get back." Satisfied, Cap picks out a shovel from the shack, shoulders it, and lumbers off towards a stand of pine trees up over the hill.

"He'll warm up once you get to know him better," Sam says watching Cap walk away with his shovel. "But he's right. We need to resupply; I can't take much more of this stuff either. Do you still have your glasses?"

"I do," I say, guiltily pulling them out from my sweatshirt.

She grabs my hand and pushes the glasses back undercover, then smiles and pats my chest. "Woah, keep those things covered up until we can use them safely, OK? It's bad enough that they track where you go. We don't need them making any more videos, right?"

I can feel my cheeks heat up as they turn red, as much from the embarrassment at the scolding as her hand on my chest. She notices and lets it linger a beat longer. I tuck the glasses back in and make a show of warming my hands on the fire.

The sun is hovering around the tree line, unable to fend off the frostiness of the morning. My breath crystallizes in front of me then floats away.

I don't know what I'm doing out here, playing a part I have no experience with. It's hard to track the series of decisions that led me into life's deepest waters. Butterflies start-up in my guts and threaten a march on my chest. I wonder what a real panic attack feels like, it can't be much different than what is brewing inside me right now.

Being with Cap and Sam is a new role for me. One I expect will be full of 'doing' rather than just 'being'. I don't feel qualified as a 'do-er' but I don't seem to have any choice in the matter.

Sam disappears into the tent and pops back out with her hair tucked tightly into the hood of her sweatshirt, large, dark sunglasses obscuring most of her face. Strapped across her shoulders is a large camouflage backpack. Something juts out against the cloth of the pack at an odd angle. She looks like a perp in a WANTED poster.

"Well, ready?" she asks, cheerily. Her demeanor has shifted considerably from our first encounter on the sidewalk when I scratched my way into her criminal enterprise, but I haven't yet developed the cynical neural pathways necessary to critically analyze her or her intentions. I want to be more in control of this situation, but I know well if she directed me to follow up my river smoothies with a meal of glass, I would fill my stomach until I shit bottles.

She doesn't wait for me to reply but starts up the bank of the valley in the opposite direction from where Cap disappeared into the trees. I follow closely, slipping on the loose leaves and pine needles, struggling to match her pace.

We reach the top of the hill where she was doing tai chi this morning, and I can see the green river winding its way through the forest. It stands eerily still, like a jagged wound on the surface of the earth filled with noxious pus, oozing its way nowhere. We head down the hill towards its banks and the smell assaults me. Sam notices my crinkled nose.

"You get used to it," she says.

I know this already. I've lived by this river for a substantial portion of my lifetime, watching the life slowly choked out of it. Adaptation is humanity's greatest offense to our scarred planet. Humans have a seemingly endless appetite for being able to live happily in our own excrement. New normals develop at break-neck speed and we find new ways to rationalize them. Progress marches on, etc., etc., etc.

Sam trots down the hill, closer to the clogged river. When we are within a dozen trees of its bank, she turns to follow the gurgling flow. She slows down and lets me pull up beside her.

"You can get used to it, but I still like to leave a buffer."

"That's why nobody used the bridge you blew up for years," I reply. "You were just as likely to pass out and fall off it if you got too close."

Sam chuckles lightly. "We overestimated the load it took to sink that thing. As weak as it was, we were lucky it didn't drag someone down with it."

We continue walking through the trees, keeping a distance from the river while following its course. I couldn't think of anything else to say. I want to make conversation and force an interaction, but my tongue stays glued to the back of my teeth. She feels no obligation to engage with me anymore, so I trudge on behind her in silence.

The sun rises higher in the sky warming the air. Breath stops freezing in white puffs in front of me. My blood is warm from the hike. I feel good. It's beautiful. I want to appreciate the moment, but a lifetime of avoiding the present makes it hard. The present is reserved for anxiety and panic. Stuck deep inside my head, I lose track of how long we move through the woods. By the time I spot a road through the branches, the sun is directly above us. Following the river becomes increasingly difficult as it bends closer towards civilization, forcing us onto the pavement to avoid the toxic green fumes.

"Where are we going?" I ask finally.

"We're getting supplies," Sam says tersely.

She stops at the edge of the pavement, looks both ways quickly then scampers across the tar. Her tone is different now than it was when she was trying to convince me to leave.

Across the pavement, she turns and looks back at me. It looks like she's calculating the distance back into cover and whether she would be able to beat me in a foot race, leaving me here on the side of the road with both thumbs up my ass. She toes the sand on her side of the road tentatively, the weight of her decision playing out across her face.

I check each way for traffic then sprint to the other side. She smiles emptily when I pull up next to her. For the first time, I note the dark circles and stress lines marking her face. She seems weighed down. I don't know if it's me or wherever we're heading.

"We need to use your glasses now. I want you to take them out from under your shirt and put them on, but do not, under any circumstances look at me when you have them on. Got it?" Sam puts her hand across the glasses where they lie across my chest. I'm sure she can feel my heart as it tries to break free from the prison of my rib cage and jump into her arms.

"I got it," I reply as coolly as possible.

"OK, put them on," she says moving her hand to my arm. "We're going to keep moving while you use them. I'll guide you along so you don't get hit by a car. Remember, do not point them at me, even in the peripherals."

She pulls on my arm and we start walking along the side of the road. With my free hand, I take the glasses out and slip them over my nose. They buzz excitedly. My vision fogs out for a second as the glasses calibrate themselves, eager to curate all the content I have been missing.

A truck rattles by us on the road and I stumble a bit in the vacuum created by its wake. She tightens her grip, steadying me.

The fog parts and the glasses settle on a steady stream of updates about the election: "Michaels Doubles Down on Chinese/Russian Threats, Promises More Jobs, Better Food. Details Plan to Fortify American Nuclear Superiority within First Sixty Days in Office."

Then: "Jones Urges Americans to Remain Calm, Trust Government."

Then: "With Pollinators Facing Extinction, US Food Supply at All-Time Low - Exacerbating Historic Famine."

Then: "Pacific Desalination Project Hits Major Roadblock, Western Water Supplies Critical."

Then: "Six New Recipes to Transform Your Go-Bars from Gross to Gourmet."

I don't browse through any of the actual articles. The order of their placement across my eyes seems to be more than the result of a random algorithm.

A car races past, tires squealing loudly as it takes a corner too fast. More headlines slip past my eyes in a blur. There appears to be no moderation or curation anymore. Information attacks my retinas.

"Can I take these off now?" I resist the urge to turn and look at Sam, to weaponize my attention.

"Hold on, OK? We need them but be careful. You've already filmed me once, remember? They'll start putting it all together if you're not careful. Come on." Sam guides my elbow as we scramble up a hill into another thick stand of pine trees. I keep the glasses trained on the ground as they hum at a low frequency, eager to be helpful.

"We're almost in the clear, just a few more minutes." Sam grabs my hand and pulls me to the top of the hill.

Below us the road and polluted river snake together towards town. Beyond the trees is a clearing and on the other side of the hill, off in the distance, are a string of dilapidated old buildings. They're arranged together in a loose circle, not like a neighborhood, more like a compound. I've never seen this part of town before.

Sam tugs my arm again and pulls me tightly to the trunk of an old-growth pine. We sit down cross-legged in the fallen leaves and needles, back to back, me facing the compound, Sam facing the road.

"Was there anything about us in those things," Sam asks.

"No. Just articles about the election and lack of food."

"Hmm," Sam scrunches up her face, "Is anyone going to miss you? Report you missing or anything?"

I pause to think it over before answering. It's the second time in the past few days someone has been interested in exactly how pathetic my life is.

Finally, I respond, "No, I don't think so. My rent is paid up for the next three weeks and my family generally leaves me alone."

I pause again and then add, "I don't have a girlfriend or anything."

I can feel my cheeks turn bright red.

"Good. Pull up the satellite view of our location. I want to know exactly where that fucker is before we go down there."

The glasses respond to my facial prompts and fill both lenses with an overhead map showing our plot. There is a lag between the glasses and the satellite, so I watch us climb the embankment and then seek cover underneath the trees. The satellites are always watching and recording, so it doesn't feel dangerous to access this information. Right now, I'm just one of the millions.

"Can you see us?" Sam asks?

"No, we're hidden." It's only a partial truth, but it makes me feel powerful not to tell her everything.

"OK, zoom in on the houses and let me know what you see."

I scrunch my nose up and the glasses intuitively respond to my command, enlarging the cluster of old buildings. I scan back and forth. Some people linger in the courtyard between the apartment building and a dilapidated barn.

"There are some people hanging around, but I don't know. Nothing weird. What exactly do you want me to look for?"

"Are they all women?"

I look closer into the glasses and count about a half dozen tiny shapes, representing people moving in, out, and between the buildings. They all look vaguely female.

"I think so, yes."

Sam grumbles, "Figures. He's probably tucked away in one of the bedrooms playing video games or something. Do you see any guns?"

Who is *he*? I squint deeply into the glasses again. "No, I don't see any guns."

Sam sighs, "Doesn't matter. Come on, let's go drop in on them. The last time I was here he was outside in some home-made shooting range showing off his arsenal. I think most of what he does is an act but Cap still almost managed to get us shot. Hopefully, they're used to me. You can tuck those things back into your shirt now."

Sam stands up behind me and I slide the glasses off. They buzz impotently against my chest - rejected again.

"You ready?" Sam asks hesitantly.

I nod, pat my chest, and force a smile.

"It's not really as bad as I just made it sound. Sorry." She laughs. "I have a tendency to be dramatic."

"It's OK. I'm not scared," I lie.

We stand looking at each other under the trees, neither one of us moving. After the longest ten seconds of my life, Sam blinks and looks down at her boots.

I think she wants me to kiss her. To sweep her off her feet and plant my tongue firmly in her mouth, claiming her as mine. She can't be happy, living in the woods with Cap, blowing up old shit for no real reason. I could take her away from this. I have some rent money saved up. We could go somewhere warm and find a way to live off the land with integrity.

She's still looking at the ground, while I make up the idea that she's nervous with desire for me. This is the moment; I think to myself. I've seen this happen in movies. For once in my stupid life, I'm ready. I take a deep breath and decide that now is the time for me to go about building the future I want to live in.

My hands move as if detached from my body. I watch in astonishment as they raise up to my shoulder level, extend off my elbows, the left wiping one lock of pink hair back off her forehead, tucking it behind her ear, the right gently cradling her chin. I can't believe I made contact with her face. Her skin is so soft, I can hardly feel it. I can't believe how well this is going.

She jolts upright at my touch. I spot a wince rise inside her. She swallows it back with obvious effort and takes my hands in hers, pulling them back down towards the space between us. The hope inside me dies, rots, and decomposes in an instant.

"That's not a good idea... not right now," she adds.

Bravery and stupidity are the Siamese twins of ambition - inoperably intertwined, fighting to the death over the ownership of my most vital organs. Each one driving the other further and further down, drowning me in a gurgling madness of confusing signals and humiliation. I let my arms fall back to my sides as they tumble out of her soft grip. My face is burning hot as the capillaries in my cheeks reach their saturation points.

"It's OK," Sam says patting my shoulder as she walks by, avoiding eye contact. "We have a lot to do."

I let her go off ahead for a dozen steps. It's painful to even look in her direction. I don't know what's happening inside me right now but it's not rational. It feels like my brain is racing out of control, spurred on by a chemical reaction deep inside my gut, unrequited love, I guess.

I press the heels of my palms into my eyes until I see stars and do my best to rub out the humiliation. With a deep breath, I push the last five minutes deep down into a dark place, chain it to a radiator, and barricade the door. It screams bloody murder and begs to be let out. I ignore its pleadings and follow Sam. She's cleared the trees and stands at the top of the hill looking down towards the little commune. She turns and smiles as I reach her side. Somewhere in the dark, a feeling inside me rattles the hinges of a locked door and demands freedom.

"Well, here we go," she says cheerily and starts off down the hill. I follow her because of course I would.

*   *   *

Two women tending a garden stop what they're doing and watch our descent. One of them stands up and says something to the other. She's older and carries an air of authority. The younger one gets up and looks worriedly in our direction. Her bright red hair burns in the morning sun. She wipes her hands on her pants, turns towards the older one briefly, and then scurries off away from us. The older woman remains standing. She moves in front of the garden and watches us close the distance down the hill.

Sam doesn't say anything, she just moves forward steadily, confident in whatever she's dragging me into. I stay far enough behind her that I don't look like a coward but leave no doubt she's going to have to navigate through this largely on her own.

We reach the bottom of the hill and the woman greets us with a forced smile. Her hair is long, reaching down to the middle of her back, it looks damaged like it's been abused by bleach for too many years. Her face is worn and wrinkled but seems kind, or simple.

"You're back," she says softly to Sam, looking past her up into the hill where we came from. "Is that black man with you?" A frown takes over her face.

"No, it's just me and my friend Jake this time," Sam replies.

The woman's face relaxes for a second, then the frown returns and deepens as she looks me up and down. "We tried to explain to you last time, you need an appointment if you want to meet with one of the girls."

"We're not looking for that," Sam says shaking her head. "I tried to explain that to you last time." She looks around the compound nervously, her voice dropping to just above a whisper, "Where is your boss?"

A door opens then crashes closed to our left as the younger girl returns followed closely by a man leaning on one crutch. A shotgun hangs across his back, connected by a leather strap. His left arm dangles from his bony shoulder.

He sticks the crutch firmly in the soft dirt, sets his feet, and unstraps the weapon on his back, raising the gun towards us with his good arm.

The older woman grabs the younger redhead by the shoulder and moves her behind the armed cripple.

"Well, well, well, look who it is," he bellows, his eyes wild with insanity. The left side of his face is frozen in a grimace. A drop of saliva falls out of the corner of his mouth. He wipes the spit away with his shoulder and waves the gun at us.

Sam puts her hands in the air and motions for me to follow suit. I take the direction.

"Felix, it's not like that. Put that thing down, we don't need to do this again."

"What're you here for this time? The produce or the pussy?" Felix laughs turn into a snarl. He grunts under the exertion of keeping the shotgun trained on us with his good hand.

"Or maybe, you've come back looking for work, eh pinky? Decided to earn an honest living?" Felix grins past the dead part of his face. The tendons in his forearm pop and twist. He won't be able to keep it up much longer. There's a decision coming, shoot us or give up. I look at Sam, she doesn't seem worried. She should be worried.

"Felix, put that thing down this is unnecessary."

"You bitch." It's his last warning. The muscles in his forearm pulse wildly as his brain sends them the command to kill. It's enough warning. I grab Sam by the backpack and swing her to the ground as Felix settles the gun on his hip and squeezes the trigger.

Sam and I hit the turf and roll to our left away from the chaos. Buckshot flies over our heads and rattles noisily against the aluminum siding on one of the buildings. There is a large crunch under my shirt as our weight and scramble crush the glasses against my chest. They vibrate wildly and then stop. The shot shatters a window and one of the women screams.

"Felix!"

I look up from my prone position, ready to fight for my life, but Felix is on his back in the middle of the garden, his feet sticking straight up like two mini gravestones. The shotgun sits smoking at his feet.

Sam locks eyes with the redhead. Panic flashes across the young woman's face as she reaches for the weapon. Sam scrambles up and dashes into the garden, arriving at the butt of the shotgun at the same moment as the redhead, pulling the barrel out of her grip and backing up. I stay firmly on the ground. I've done enough for one afternoon.

Felix looks up from his ruins and groans. The older woman wraps her arms around his chest and props him up. The three of them sit watching us. I can see movement in the windows of the buildings around us. Sam points the gun at them.

"Don't move."

A window flies opens on the second floor of the old farmhouse to our right. The muzzle of some ancient-looking gun juts out, behind it a blonde woman with a plain face sticks her head out the opening.

"Felix, you want I should kill these ones too?" she yells, her voice ringing off the walls like the buckshot.

Felix laughs loudly, yelling back, "No, not these ones ... for some silly reason, these ones apparently want to live."

The blonde squints her eyes at us then reluctantly pulls her weapon and face back inside the building. The window stays open.

"It's a single shot," Felix says, waving his good hand dismissively at Sam as she lowers the shotgun. He turns to the women and laughs with resignation. "Almost got 'em." He picks his lifeless hand up with his good arm and lets it drop back into the dirt.

Sam breaks down the gun, checking to see if there is another shell in the breach. It's empty. She tosses it aside and gives me a hand up off the grass. Felix sits on his damaged haunches with a bemused look on his face.

The older woman eyes me with a naked hatred. The young redhead sniffs loudly, pulling the snot from a fledgling cold back into her face. Composed she stares through me. Their withering gazes bear down on me.

I know what this place is. I know why Cap wouldn't come back. I know it because I can see my reflection in their faces. To them, I am the physical manifestation of everything terrible, an animal that does nothing but walks, talks, eats, shits, and fucks. I kill and consume and destroy then breed creatures similar to myself, equally disgusting only smaller, teaching them to follow in my footsteps. It becomes impossible to look any of them in their eyes.

"You're a mad man, Felix. Truly mad." Anger is splashed across Sam's face in hot crimson streaks.

"What did you come to steal this time? My food or my women?" Felix sneers, spittle piling up in the lame corner of his mouth.

Sam blushes again but remains assertive, "We need more food. And this time we're not stealing anything," she adds.

The older woman dabs at Felix's lips, cleaning up the spittle. He looks at her thankfully then gently pushes her hand away. "I don't suppose you brought anything useful, like money, did you? Or maybe you would prefer a trade?" He can't help himself, a small pink tongue darts out of Felix's mouth, rolling suggestively across his withered lips.

"Fuck you, Felix." The air flows out of Sam's lungs in a rush. She looks rattled, ready to fight, like a tea kettle boiling over.

"Well ...?" Felix asks with a glint in his eye.

Sam takes a deep breath, refilling her chest with air, and then lets it back out. She flexes her fingers, opening and closing small fists. The anger dissipates little by little with each new inhale.

"We brought cash. Old school."

"Let's see it," Felix responds warily.

Sam slings the pack back over her shoulder, unzips it, and produces a wad of bills. She fans them with her thumb for Felix to inspect.

"Well, why didn't you say so? So rare to have someone want to pay in hard currency anymore. Still, it makes the world go 'round, doesn't it?" Felix guffaws. "Fetch my crutch, won't you dear?" He points towards the younger woman.

Dutifully, the redhead retrieves it from the dirt and returns it to her pimp, picking him up off the ground gently and dusting him off. Upright again, Felix slips the crutch under his left armpit and points his crooked finger at the lump on my chest.

"What is under his shirt?"

My injured glasses buzz meekly giving themselves away.

"That's what I thought," Felix crows. "In the box."

The older woman materializes a small metal box from seemingly nowhere and opens it to me. Dutifully, I slip the glasses over my head, fold them up, and place them inside. The frames are twisted and one of the lenses is missing. They're useless. She closes the box with a snap and quickly disappears it back into the folds of her clothes.

"Follow me," Felix commands, ambling off towards the run-down barn with his broken gait.

There is movement all around us now. Shadows slip menacingly in the windows of the buildings that ring the small courtyard.

Swiveling on my heels, I do my best to take stock of all the activity above us. There is too much to keep track of. The sensation of being watched is palpable, it makes the hair on the back of my neck stand up. I scan the dark windows again, expecting to see another gun muzzle sticking through. Shapes move around hazily but I can't make out any concrete threats.

Sam has followed Felix towards the barn and is already twenty yards ahead of me. Goosebumps ripple across my flesh as my bones protest further involvement with these people. Terrified, my feet stick to the garden dirt like they are buried in concrete. Sam pauses and turns over her shoulder towards me.

"Come on, it's ok," she says unconvinced.

My mouth is dry. Felix and his two whores stop and turn around to watch. With the empty shotgun still lying at my feet, I shake my head towards Sam "no".

"One second," she says to Felix as she jogs back towards me.

"So sensitive," Felix responds mockingly, a sly grin starting high on the good side of his lip, cutting across his face like a stab wound.

Sam reaches out and takes me by the hand, "Come on, let's finish this and get out of here. Be strong. Pretend like they're harmless."

I am unconvinced - thoroughly.

She runs her thumb softly across the back of my hand and tugs me gently towards the group and softly repeats, "Come on."

Energy passes from her hand, routed by my heart throughout my body, shattering the concrete binding my feet firmly to the earth. I move forward, led by the hand like a small child being dragged reluctantly into the doctor's office by a patient mother - with pink hair.

Felix watches our dance with the sloped grin still slashed across his face. As we approach, he turns with the women, passing through the doors of the large dilapidated barn. We follow behind them, stopping a few feet past the entrance. The barn is one large open room, at least two stories tall. The roof has two large rectangular holes cut into it, covered by semi-opaque sheeting illuminating the room with natural light. Hoses snake along the walls, feeding sprinkler heads affixed in neat two-foot intervals on the rafters.

The floor of the barn is bare earth, with rows after row of plants sticking out of the dirt. Women, dressed in shabby jeans and old dresses, meander amongst the rows, tending to the vegetables.

Felix hobbles down the center, dragging his useless leg through the garden, looking left and right in quick succession, nodding his approval, or stopping to quickly point out an area for improvement. The women move around behind him, keeping their eyes on the soil, focusing on their work, pausing briefly to acknowledge Felix, accepting his praise, or a suggestion as he walks by.

On one side are walls of corn stalks at least as tall as me. Spindly, vine-y plants holding small gourds wind their way through the bottom of the corn maze. On the other side, dozens of circular wire scaffolds support tomato plants, heavy with red and green fruit. The barn is teeming with food.

I didn't think places like this existed anymore. I don't know how he could possibly have been permitted for this or bought this much seed undetected on the black market. My head swoons as I try to take it all in. All seed has been regulated since I was a little kid, carefully controlled and distributed through strict permitting. The bright colors of the vegetable and the fruit are overwhelming. It feels like walking onto an alien planet.

"It's amazing isn't it?" Sam asks, looking around, still clutching my hand.

Small flocks of sparrows and finches circle the space above our heads, hopping noisily from one rafter to another, waiting for an opportunity to swoop in and steal a bit of greenery. Sam and I stare at the scene in wonder.

"It was worth coming back to see this again," Sam says, her chest rising and falling in a deep sigh of contentment.

She looks at me and then down at our hands and releases, her face red with embarrassment.

Felix has made his way to the end of the barn. "This way," he gurgles at us over the din, motioning for us to follow while leaning heavily on his single crutch.

We pick our way carefully through the delicate rows of plants and chirping birds. The women continue with their work around us, being sure not to look up at us or make eye contact. To them, seeing Sam must be like a Chihuahua confronting a wolf in the wild - untamed, collarless with the taste of raw meat still on its breath. I can almost see them quaking in her presence.

"Corn is $20 a stalk. Tomatoes are $15 each. We have sweet potatoes and russet; they are both $10 a pound. Cucumbers, squash, and pumpkins are $8 a pound. And before you ask, we don't sell any of our seed," Felix says over his shoulder. He pauses for a second and adds, "Pussy is $500 an hour, one hour minimum, or they'll use their hand on you for $100, but you don't get to be alone." He waits for another beat. I can feel my skin crawling as another grin spreads across his crooked mouth. "No? What about you Pink-y?" he motions towards Sam.

"We're here for the food, Felix," she replies.

Felix chuckles through a hacking cough. "Ok, we'll see then. This way." He continues shuffling ahead of us, dragging his broken body out of the garden room, then stops and turns back to us. "Forgive me, but I just remembered, it's $50 pre-paid just to see the produce."

Sam sighs and peels off a bill from her stack, handing it towards Felix. The older woman intercepts it quickly, tucking the money into a pocket hidden in her blouse. Satisfied, he starts walking away again.

We follow him through a window-less hallway with a dirt floor that has a slight downward slope. Deeper into his lair we go. Bare bulbs ring the low ceiling in sporadic intervals, cones of light spreading then fading quickly as we follow Felix and his women underground.

No one talks, the only sound is that of our shuffling feet. Gone is the wonder of the colorful splendor in the garden. Everything down here is muted and ugly. I nudge Sam gently with my elbow and give her my best "this seems like a good way to get killed, doesn't it?" look. She seems worried and reads my concern immediately but makes a silent play of this being a perfectly normal thing to do.

The sudden mind-meld does nothing to slow our willing descent into whatever death trap Felix has devised underground. As we pass from open bulb to open bulb, the scenarios for all the ways this could go poorly play out across the neurotic recesses of my skull. Every disaster scenario revolves around women with pinched faces, loose morals, and itchy trigger fingers. The options are endless.

The air in the tunnel smells stale with earth, it tickles my nose building up a sneeze that starts, stops, and dies. By the time the path ends at another door, the other end of the tunnel has long disappeared.

The door is thick and wooden, apparently a remnant from a long-forgotten, cold war bomb shelter. A large cast-iron padlock dangles menacingly off the latch. The old woman takes out a key from some secret pocket, opens the padlock, and pushes through the door. She flips on a light illuminating a giant round room with old wooden barrels and bins ringing the walls. We move together as a group into the center of the circle. The ceiling extends thirty feet upwards, culminating in a small pinnacle of sunlight streaming through a cap in the ground above us.

Vertigo overtakes me and I look down to avoid passing out. Sam notices and steadies me with a hand on my shoulder, determined, apparently, to walk me through this.

The synapses in my head reconnect and the pieces of my sight come back together like a puzzle. Sam lets me go and walks around the room inspecting their produce.

She digs into a bin of tomatoes pulling out a dozen. Even from a distance, I can see dark spots sticking out amongst the red and the green. She moves to another bin and pulls out five large russet potatoes, then five sweet potatoes from a third, dark spots and green eyes ring those as well.

She places the haul carefully on the dirt floor and moves around the other bins; a dozen mushy apples from one, four ears of corn with grey husks. Sam searches the bins one more time then returns to the pile of quickly rotting vegetables, opening her pack.

Felix clicks his tongue on the roof of his mouth. "Is that it?" he asks, raising his eyebrows into an arc around his frozen face.

"Felix, all this here is a bunch of shit," Sam says pushing around some of the apples with a foot. "It's practically compost. Expensive compost at those prices."

"Yes, well, as you may have noticed, there's a bit of a shortage going on at the moment and well the market dictates, doesn't it my dear?"

Sam frowns and rolls one of the moldy sweet potatoes into a smoldering tomato. "Do you have any meat?" she asks.

"No."

Sam's shoulder slump, "This isn't like last time."

The older woman hunches down and counts the haul at Sam's feet. Her mouth moves silently as she calculates the math in her head. She counts them again; double-checking then stands up and says "$350."

Sam shakes her head. "Cap is not going to like this extortion."

"Something tells me you can afford it, right?" Felix says. "It pays to be above the law, doesn't it?"

The comment lands on Sam like a punch. She flinches as her spine stiffens.

Felix watches, delighted to have pierced her armor, managing even to nudge the dead left corner of his mouth.

"I see everything around here girlie. I see you roll into town one day and find my little operation immediately. Then I see you running around on TV blowing things to smithereens and a few days later you brazenly show up back here."

Felix pauses and searches Sam's face for a reaction. "These are strange times we live in, aren't they dear?"

A long pause hangs awkwardly between them, sucking the air out of the room.

"Are you finished?" Sam asks.

"Oh, I see, you're right in the middle of something, aren't you? Well then, I guess we are finished. I have never been one to stand in the way of progress, you know. Best of luck to you both," he cackles loudly.

Everyone is looking at me and I don't know why. Life seems to happen around me, like a powerful river flowing through a dead tree stump.

Sam stoops down, picks up the vegetables, and scoops them into her bag. She peels off most of the bills from her stack and hands them towards Felix. The older woman intercepts the cash again and disappears it into the folds of her outfit. The full pack sags heavily across Sam's small back. I reach for it and she gratefully hands it over to me.

"How do we get out of here?" Sam asks.

Felix leans on his crutch and points up towards the grey skylight. The younger woman moves to the wall and unwraps a rope from a metal cleat. Overheads a series of pulleys groan against their rusted parts. The redhead holds onto the rope, letting it out slowly as a large wooden platform lowers from the ceiling. The grain elevator looks like an oversized dumb waiter.

"You go up, we go out. Climb on then," he says waving a hand dismissively at us.

Sam steps on the platform and waits for me. This seems like insanity. I need to break the water flowing around me before I drown.

"How are we supposed to get to the top?" I ask.

"He speaks!" Felix exclaims. "How wonderful my boy, and to think I figured you as nothing more than an elaborate flesh and blood puppet. A dumb mute. But you speak!" Felix winks at the older whore.

She pulls a small handgun from another pocket hidden in her frock and hands it to him. Felix taps the gun against his crutch and motions for me to move on.

"Why you stand on it and use those muscles to pull on the rope and it magically pulls you straight up. Then you climb out through the cupola, get the fuck off my property, and never return. Do you understand now? Do you?"

The gun looks old and foreign, belonging to another time and place. Felix aims it at my head, cocks it, and smiles. "Do you?" he repeats again.

I follow his directions, climb onto the platform next to Sam, and pause. Something is gnawing at me.

"Can I have my glasses?" I ask.

"Your glasses? Is that it? Why of course! What would I want with those wretched things?"

The box appears magically from another pocket and is placed on the platform at my feet. Felix grins and waves, "Goodbye."

Sam grasps the rope dangling from the ceiling and begins to pull. "Come on," she says, "Let's get out of here."

I take a grip with both hands above hers and we pull down together. The platform lurches off the ground. One by one, we reach for handful after handful of rope and carefully navigate up towards the light. The rusty infrastructure creaks in protest at each pull but the bead of sun gets bigger and bigger.

At the top is a cleat and we tie the rope off securing the platform. The hole in the ceiling is a five-foot square. Sam bends down using her hands to help push my feet up as I maneuver my carcass back out into the yard.

Reaching down, I grab Sam's arm and pull her out of the hole. We have reappeared a few hundred yards away from where we first approached the compound. Sam helps me up and we brush the dirt off ourselves, avoiding eye contact. Back by the barn, a dozen dusty looking women have gathered to watch us go. I spot dark shapes moving again in the windows above.

"Let's go," Sam says through clenched teeth and starts back up the hill away from the ring of crusty buildings.

A window cracks in the apartment building next to us and Felix's admonition not to kill us yet rattles through my head like a pinball. I close the five-step head-start Sam has in two leaping gallops and pass her up the hill at a dead sprint. My feet flail desperately for traction amongst the fallen leaves and dead grass as my lungs scream in protest, unprepared for their sudden call to action. Fear feeds adrenaline, pushing my feeble muscles to their shredding point. Ten more agonizing steps and I reach the top of the hill, throwing myself over the peak and army crawl back into the cover of a stand of trees.

I take the backpack off, careful not to damage the rotting produce, then unceremoniously throw up into a small puddle of leafy, dirty water.

A hazy refection of a pained, scared man peers up at me through chunks of Go-Bars and waterlogged worms. I consider the mirror for a minute and then contribute all remaining food-like substances and stomach bile to the growing stew floating beneath my arms.

If pain is really just weakness leaving the body, then pain tastes just like nacho cheese and acid. Reaching my hands into my pockets, I pull the shattered glasses out and examine them. They're destroyed, so I toss them into the woods - a proper burial.

*   *   *

The day is cool, especially in the shade of the trees, but sweat stains already stand out through my shirt. I feel overheated, over-stimulated, and over-stressed. Sam leans casually against a tree, watching as another heave rattles up from my ragged skeleton, sending a final, meager stream of vomit up, out and into the puddle. I wait for a second, then wipe my nose with my sleeve and flip onto my back.

The sun hangs low in the sky, threatening to dip below the tree line. A deep purple dusk sits just out of reach, waiting for its turn to take over. I want to lie here and let the darkness cover me like a blanket. I can't believe I ever complained about my life before this mess. It's only been a day, but I would give anything to go back to designing forks and playing video games in my decrepit little apartment. I wonder if I still can.

"Are you Ok?" Sam asks after a moment.

I lift my chin up and look down past my toes. She smiles and walks over, extending a hand to help me off the ground.

"That was exciting, wasn't it?" she asks laughing. "Thanks for pushing me out of the way of that shot. That was pretty badass."

"You're welcome." I take her hand, shaking my head and stand up woozily - understatements and such. Sam crouches down in the leaves and opens the pack. She rifles through the produce and emerges with two soft apples.

"These are the best-looking ones of the bunch," she says sheepishly, handing one to me.

I take the fruit, consider a brown spot the size of my thumb then take a generous bite from the opposite side. The flesh is mealy but it's sweet and helps wash the taste of throw up out of my mouth. Sam watches me eat, only nibbling at hers. I pick the last pieces of apple flesh off the core and then toss the rest into the woods.

Sam's eyes stay fixated on me. Her gaze is uncomfortable. Self-consciously, I raise the hood over my head and tighten the drawstrings around my forehead.

"What do you think, Jake? Is this for you?"

My weaknesses are obvious, worn on my sleeves like the wiped-away puke. I turn away from Sam with crossed arms and reconsider the life awaiting me back in my cold little apartment. It was the life of a goldfish, swimming in my own shit, waiting for some big hand, cloaked in mystery, to dispense food, hopefully at regular intervals.

"It's OK to admit if it's not. This is a different thing than you're used to. If you want, I'll show you to the road and then you can get on back to town," she says to my back.

I don't respond but stoop to pick up the pack, shoulder it, and turn back towards Sam. Her eyes pick up the meager sunlight, amplifying it and sparkle with fire. She stands in front me amongst the grey death and decay of oncoming winter and shines like a small pink bomb of life, helpless to do anything but messily explode over everything. I absorb her and remind myself I saved her life today. I can do this and the only thing worse than following her would be leaving.

With a forced smile painted across my face, I summon the steel to swallow my fear and respond "I'm Ok. Let's head back to camp. There is work to do." Even to me, my voice sounds watery and unconvincing.

Sam leans against a tree and looks me over skeptically. I stand as confidently as I can and weather the assault.

"Alright," she says with a shrug and a sigh. "Let's go," and we make our way back down the other side of the hill.

CHAPTER SEVEN

I Like Mike

We walk back in silence, Sam leading the way following the road along where it parallels the green, dead river. The backpack full of vegetables is heavy on my back, and my mind is focused on the decision I made to stay. The thought of returning to the camp and dealing with Cap brings panic to the edge of my throat, but it would take more courage than I can muster to change my mind and leave.

Head down, I brood over the decision, watching Sam's heels as we pass over gravel elbows and piles of mushy wet leaves. The sun drops behind the tree line and the air cools. The smell from the river is muted by the crispness of dusk. Streetlights flicker on, humming with a yellow glow.

A voice breaks out behind us, making me flinch in surprise. "Hello, Brother! Hello, Sister! Do you have a minute to discuss the future of our great country?"

Two young men pop out from a perpendicular road full of run-down apartment buildings. They must have been going door-to-door and spotted us when we passed. Without a car or the plausible deniability afforded by a door and a deadbolt, we are sitting ducks.

Both are blond with earnest blue eyes and red cheeks. They're wearing the familiar uniform, bland clothing of jeans and white shirts, and carrying *Michaels for President* branded sweatshirts across their shoulders. They aren't quite twins, but they could be brothers.

Sam turns and shoots me a look to let her handle this. The boys look up and down the road in unison, searching for traffic and then scurry across, stopping in front of us. Each one holds a binder with an 'I Like Mike' sticker on it. They smile at us, straining to appear casual and friendly. Concern clouds their eyes as they take us in.

"Hi friends! What are you doing out alone in the cold?" The brothers frown in unison, puzzled by our alienness.

" Just enjoying some fresh air," Sam replies, voice dripping with fake peppiness.

They look at me to see if I agree it is possible to enjoy evening air that stinks of decay and death.

"Uhh, me too," I add quickly, backing up Sam.

"Ok, well, my name's Jasper..."

"And I'm Paul."

"As you probably know, there's quite an important election coming up in a few days..."

"Probably the most important ever."

"Right, the most important ever. And we're very concerned about what is happening in the world..."

"Horrible things," Paul emphasizes solemnly.

"Yes, horrible things and we feel like it's time to prioritize America, which is why we're supporting Mike Michaels. He might not have the coolest name, but he's the best choice."

They both chuckle lightly, pleased with the humility of their small joke. They stop laughing and wait for our reaction, concerned at first then relieved as Sam and I force smiles.

"So, you may have seen some troubling stories in the news," Jasper continues, warping his face into an exaggerated frown.

"I haven't seen anything," Sam interjects cheerily, trying to push the interaction to a conclusion.

"Oh, really?" Jasper says confused, "you don't follow the news?"

"Well I see it sometimes on my phone or on my glasses, but I try not to read it. It's usually too upsetting...and full of lies," Sam looks at me.

"Uhh, me too," I add agreeably.

The boys pause, bottom lips tucked pensively underneath their front teeth in twin expressions of apprehension. Sam smiles, raising her eyebrows innocently. They look us over one more time then the black cloud lifts off their faces.

"Great!" Paul exclaims, "Do you guys want some stickers?"

"You bet we do!" Sam replies, raising her chin towards me.

"Um, yeah, sounds awesome," I muster.

Jasper digs through his folder, produces two identical, blue, and yellow 'I Like Mike' stickers and hands them over to us.

"You guys have a super night, Ok? We've got to get going. We have a few more stops on our route. Mike appreciates your support."

Sam and I stand under the flickering streetlight watching the two of them happily march away from us, down another street lined by old sagging apartment buildings, their heads robotically whipping left and right searching for any signs of life in the windows they pass. We watch them until they are absorbed into the encroaching night and fade out of sight.

A wind picks up. It swirls through the trees, rattling the bare branches, lifting the smell of green death from the river, and drenching us in its horrifying perfume. The stench enters our skulls through nostrils before settling across our brains, pickling every thought in a vile marinade.

Sam takes a deep breath then lets it out with a sigh. I stand beside her stupidly frozen in place. The silence continues between us fighting for airspace with the river stink. Her shoulders slump as she traces a line in the gravel with one small shoe.

"Let's go," she says finally without looking up.

Again, I find myself without any better ideas and follow behind, the lost dog, as she picks her way down the path back towards camp.

CHAPTER EIGHT

Chicken Shit

I smell the fire before I see it. We feel our way up the last hill in the pitch black and look down in the ravine at Cap sprawling in front of a sputtering campfire. Sam pauses at the crest and we watch him feed more sticks into the struggling flames. As he moves around, his massive frame throws monstrous shadows across the campground.

Cap pauses, log in hand, cocks his head slightly over his shoulder and booms, "I ain't some animal in a zoo. Might as well get your gawking asses down here." He lets the wood fall out of his grip into the flames.

Sparks fly up over his head, desperate for some escape from this hell. Finding none, they die quickly and float back to earth like black snow. A pocket of sap boils then pops, sending another round of doomed astronauts into the atmosphere. Cap settles back in his chair and watches.

We stay transfixed in place above him watching as he picks a plastic jug of water off the ground, tilts it back, and drinks deeply. Satisfied, he lowers the jug and belches. Sam checks in on me and I respond with a half nod, half-shrug. She smiles falsely and starts down the hill. Cap hears us coming and turns to watch as we move out of the darkness and into the circle of light thrown off by the fire.

"Hi," Sam greets him as we approach.

"You both make it back?" he asks with mock wonder, "That's a surprise." Cap nods towards the pack heavy on my back, "What'd you get?"

I un-shoulder the bag and drop it at his feet, then take a spot around the fire. I collapse into the flimsy chair with a bone-tiredness. Sam approaches with another jug of water and drops it gently in my lap. I take a grateful gulp, watching as Cap hunches over the bag and inventories our haul from Felix. He finishes his sorting and sits back in the chair.

"How much did you pay for this shit?"

"Don't ask. Too much," Sam replies. The stress of the day is carved across her face, deepening the stress lines. She stares into the fire rubbing her temples with the index fingers on each hand. Her mouth is open, popping her jaw back and forth. Cap watches her while chewing unhappily on his toothpick. I can see his mind processing how hard to push.

"This is a bunch of shit," Cap picks up a moldering tomato and drops it back into the pack. He looks aggressively from Sam to me, waiting for someone to take responsibility for his ruined meal. I'm too drained to care about his bluster. Ignoring him, I prod the burning logs with a long, thin stick. Sam watches me fiddle, continuing her deadpan.

Cap lets out a defeated "motherfucker" under his breath. His shoulders slump, and he drapes his massive arms across his knees, head down, face covered by dreadlocks, defeated. I get up and drop another log into the fire. We watch as flames first lick the log then explode into the cold night air.

Cap claps his hands suddenly, grabs the pack, and heads back towards the shanty. He re-emerges shortly holding three potatoes wrapped in tin foil and three ears of corn still in the husks, placing them on a rock ringing the fire.

"Nothin' to do but make chicken shit out of chicken shit," Cap says gruffly settling back into his seat. He reaches over, takes the stick out of my hand, and rotates the bounty as it cooks. A little cigar emerges from behind his left ear. He lights it on the glowing end of the stick, pulls deeply, and relaxes.

"Fuck."

Smoke billows out from Cap's nostrils as his mouth releases his innermost thoughts.

I catch Sam's eye and she smiles.

"I hate this place." Cap rolls the ears of corn over with his stick. One of the husks has caught fire. It smells like marijuana as it burns.

More spark explorers pop and fly off into the atmosphere. I sit back on the chair with my arms over my head and watch the little balls of fire dance their dying jig. I wonder what Cap means by "this place?" The ravine we're stuck in or a bigger picture? It doesn't make sense, them here, blowing up aging infrastructure. Neither one of them is from this place, and I have a feeling that we should move on before the cold makes this little campsite intolerable.

I look over at Sam, her eyes are closed but her face has relaxed in the warmth of the fire. Cap sucks on his cigar as he cooks my well-earned dinner. He catches me looking and extends one large middle finger in my direction.

CHAPTER NINE

Saying What You Mean

The first rays of sunlight start to penetrate the thick blackness of the ravine, and I hear Sam stirring in her tent. Away from the protective halo of the fire, I spent another night holed up on the floor of the rickety shack, sleeping fitfully in stops and starts.

I hear a zip as Sam emerges from the tent heading towards the hill, probably for another round of tai-chi or whatever it is I saw her doing the first morning. I make a show of rustling in my bag as she gets closer, signaling I am awake too. Sam stops and knocks politely on the side of the shack.

"You awake?" she asks quietly.

I quickly sit up and smile, proving my lucidity.

Sam bends down on her haunches and taps my legs. "Come with me, let's talk."

My heart races, beating furtively against its cage of bone. I quickly fumble out of the sleeping bag and lace up my shoes. It's been three days since I changed my clothes. My skin and hair feel slick with my own filth. There is no mirror to reveal the true depths of my uncleanliness, but from the amount of fine ash from the fire on my arms, I can make a strong estimation that I am not a pretty sight. Sam, through whatever pixie magic she possesses, looks clean and fresh and beautiful.

She stands up smiling and nods her head up towards the top of the hill, then disappears out of the doorway. I scramble the rest of the way out of my sleeping bag and scurry to catch up with her. She stops at the crest with her hands on her hips observing the new morning as it slowly illuminates the forest.

Ignoring me, she takes off her sweatshirt. Down to a sports bra again, she begins rotating through the waist while conducting a complicated series of rhythmic motions with her arms. Her eyes are closed tight, and each breath is controlled. She breathes in deeply through her nose and out slowly through pursed lips.

Emboldened by her deep concentration, I let my eyes wander over her body. They linger at her chest, pupils widening to let in as much of the early morning light as possible. I stare hard and make out a faint outline of nipples standing out in the cold against the faint pink fabric of her bra. She lets the air out her lungs in a long hiss and I look up finding her eyes open and aware of my leering.

My face turns red and I turn away to look out across the horizon.

"Have you figured out why are you here, Jake? Why are you out in the middle of the woods, eating bad food, sleeping on the ground? What's in this for you?"

Still recovering from embarrassment, I can't bear to look at her yet. I shrug my shoulders, "I don't know. Nothing else was going right for me."

Sam presses on. "I think you do know why you're here. I think you have something in mind and you're too afraid to ask."

I watch her shadow leap across the ground in chunky choreographed movements and consider her statement. There is a thing I want very badly and am afraid to ask for. I want her. She must sense that on some level, that I am in love with her. Up to this point, my life has been pointless, filled with a suffocating loneliness. My only motivation has been to find and finance intricate distractions to keep me from falling into the hole that opened inside me.

There is risk here. I can't tell how leading her questions are. I look up into her eyes to see if they contain any hints about what she wants me to say. She stares back blankly, waiting to see what I will do.

I look down quickly and toe the dirty leaves at my feet. Sam's shadow keeps performing its intricate dance across the hill. My mouth feels like cotton. I open and close it dumbly trying to drum up the courage to speak for myself. My heart races, flooding my veins with adrenaline, adding to the discomforting feeling of wanting to run screaming away from her and towards her at the same time.

Sam stops her routine and takes my hand in hers, lifting my eyes away from my feet.

"Just say it," she coos. "Why are you really here?"

A gurgling starts somewhere low in my guts, building steam as it races up through twenty feet of intestines, bumping and scraping against the walls of my stomach, before slamming through my esophagus and launching itself past my lips manifesting as "I love you." My teeth snap twice trying vainly to grab the words and shove them back down where they came from.

Sam flinches as my words bombard her. She recovers quickly with a confused but polite smile. It's too late. Her natural reaction is crushing. She clears her throat. "What?" she asks gracefully, trying to give me a way out.

The strength in my knees starts to melt and I look sheepishly around for some way to escape. Maybe a stick sturdy and sharp enough to impale myself on. Perhaps a rock with enough fortitude to crack my skull. All I can find are dead leaves and twigs. There is no easy way out.

Out of options, I repeat "What?" back to her, my voice cracking with uncleared phlegm.

Sam pushes through, "Jake, I told you from the beginning if you stayed, I was going to ask something of you. Don't you want to do something, to say something, to really live."

These are the things I want desperately, but I can't articulate them anymore completely than a clumsy, "I love you." Sam gives up on finishing her exercises.

She hesitates, unsure of how to proceed. I do my best to continue avoiding eye contact. The mortification seeps its way through my veins, digging into the marrow of my bones. I keep my mouth closed. I just want whatever this is to end.

Unwilling to give up, Sam reaches down, with visible effort, and takes my hands in hers. She pulls them towards her and motions for me to look up. This is supposed to be comforting, but the obvious effort it takes her to touch me like this just makes the feelings of isolation and embarrassment worse. Sensing the tension in my arms she starts gently rubbing the backs of my hands with her thumbs and drops her head down to meet my eye level.

"Cap and I can't just stay out here sleeping in the woods for no reason. We've been waiting around for too long now. It's time to get moving again, and if you want to stay, you have to prove you're with us. We're here to accomplish something very specific. I can't tell you what it is yet. You need to show me, us, you're committed. Do you understand? Are you going to be with us?"

I don't understand, but I don't know how to effectively communicate my stupidity any better than I already have.

"I want you to tell me what you want. I can't do it for you." Sam coaxes my eyes up towards her then looks anxiously over my shoulder. Cap has managed to silently climb up our side of the hill and is leaning against a tree behind me, chewing absently on a Go-Bar. He plops the last chunk of compressed sawdust into his mouth, fishes a knife off his belt, and begins working the dirt out from underneath his fingernails.

"Don't mind me," he encourages as the silence stretches on.

Sam draws my attention back to her. "What do you want to do?"

There is clearly only one acceptable answer to this question, so I give up and let myself fall into it, like an actor playing a role, "I want to burn it down."

Sam's face lightens and her mouth twists into a smile. "What do you want to burn down?"

"All of it." That seems like the most appropriate answer, something my new character, Anarchist Man, would say.

Sam runs her tongue across her lips and laughs excitedly. "Exactly, but where should we start. We have to have a starting place."

The answer is easy, but I pause and make a play of dramatically considering the options. "The Mike Michaels' campaign center."

Sam looks to Cap briefly then shakes her head up and down joyously. "That's a great choice."

A smile breaks across my face. Never have my words had this superpower: this is the first time I have ever made Sam happy.

Cap folds up the knife and sticks it back in his belt. His lips are pursed, and his face is dour. "That's what you want to do? Blow something else the-fuck up?"

The smile fades from Sam's face. "I think that's a great choice. Those bastards have it coming, you know? We could make a really great statement. Let them know we're here and we won't stand for this. That we aren't sheep; we can fight. Someone has to stop them from ending the world." She looks towards me encouragingly.

"Yeah." Cap pauses, looks over us holding hands and smiling. His eyes harden and anger flashes, "Y'all motherfuckers ..." he stops himself, shakes his head, and starts back off down the hill.

Sam watches him as he works his way back to camp, stopping to pick up sticks along the way to feed into the fire. He settled into a seat around the rocks with his back to us. She turns her face towards me, eyes swimming with excitement again,

"Come, we have a lot of planning to do."

CHAPTER TEN

Life

The bag of food we brought back from Felix's had turned into a mushy paste of goo. Cap spent the last two days picking through it unhappily, muttering to himself. I managed another apple before they went to complete shit, but most of my calories have come from the seemingly never-ending supply of nutrient-rich Go-Bars.

A beard is growing in thickly around my neck and lips, the coarse hair blackened from nights sitting by the fire. The hair on my head has matted with grease and filth, and I've grown comfortable accepting my single pair of underwear as a second skin, so much that the thought of peeling it off my thighs brings a shudder.

I've lost track of how long I've been out in the wilderness. Somehow Sam has managed to avoid the choking filth that has taken over me. I've mostly kept quiet observing the dynamic between her and Cap. Sam is like a judo master, deftly side-stepping Cap's anger, using his momentum against him to accomplish the tasks she wants done.

The plan, settled on quickly, is to build a "mobile explosive device" and place it "strategically" so that the entire building is demolished. Their plans are confusing, and I listen only half interested.

I still don't know any more about either of them than I did when we first met. How they ended up together in the farthest northeast corner of the country, rattling crusty infrastructure, is a nagging detail I choose to avoid confronting directly.

I can feel the tenuousness of the house of cards on which I am now propped. It seems like acknowledging the obvious would only serve to hasten my tumble back to earth. Inside me, there is still the irresistible pull towards Sam. Separating myself from her at this point is like a fish wishing it had legs. You can't wish evolution into happening. She holds an un-rectifiable advantage in the power dynamic between us.

My main motivation during the past two days of planning and sitting around has been to not make a nuisance of myself. It seems important to Sam that I oversee and, in some way, approve of whatever plans they craft, but it is clear I am not an important cog in the machine. Teams require Indians, not just chiefs, I guess.

"We have to go back into town," Sam announces, "After breakfast," she adds with a smile.

Cap has turned largely silent, expressing his feelings with glares and sharp sighs. He doesn't bother to look up during Sam's announcement. Instead, he opens a nacho Go-Bar, throws the wrapper into the fire, and watches as it smokes and curls in the heat.

"What're we up to?" I ask, cringing at the choice of words. I sound like a kid asking about weekend plans.

"We need to scope out the site, plan our entry and exit. All that kind of stuff," she replies, ignoring my awkwardness.

"Man are you stupid or what?" Cap booms out of nowhere, his head snapping to attention. He startles me in the middle of a pull from the water jug and I spill it down my chin and the front of my shirt. This serves as an appropriate answer to his question.

He turns to Sam. "This is how you want to do it, huh? Any poor, corny motherfucker will do?"

"Cap, come on. Not now," Sam pleads, her face flushed with embarrassment.

Cap scoffs. "This one is you Sam. Just remember that. This one is *all* you."

Sam turns away from the two of us and stomps back towards her tent. I stay seated, water dribbling off my chin.

Cap lowers his voice. "You know she's playing you, don't you? You're not that blind, you can't be."

I do know this. Or at least I suspect it. "Maybe, but it's nice to be involved in something important."

"Yeah, something important. Man, you are stupid." He lowers his voice and looks at me earnestly for the first time. "Listen to me, you'll get trapped in this and then they'll never let you go."

I wipe my chin, look away from Cap and start fiddling with the cap on the water jug. I don't know who 'they' is.

Hopefully, he'll just leave me alone. The tent unzips and Sam emerges with her backpack on. She looks at me and smiles.

"Ready to go?" she asks.

I stand and brush off my pants.

Cap bristles visibly and raises his hands dismissively. "Ya'll just go out on your date or whatever the fuck it is you think you're doing."

Sam stands in front of him with her hands on her hips. Cap stays seated staring coolly into the fire, another toothpick has appeared, and he passes it back and forth between the corners of his mouth. With both hands, Sam tucks her hair up into a neat bun and turns away with a sigh. I follow her out of the camp as she moves in and out of the trees, tracking an unseen trail by memory. "What did he say to you?" she asks finally.

"Nothing," I quickly reply.

Sam looks at me skeptically.

"He said you were using me and then he swore a couple of times, nothing major."

"Uh-huh, do you think I'm using you?"

"I don't know ... maybe. I'm not sure what I have that you would want and either way I guess I don't mind. It's nice ... you know ... just to be around you, I guess." It sounds squishy but it's the most direct I can be.

A shallow smile pulls on Sam's cheeks. "We have to keep our pace up. Lots to do today."

I feel my spine wrench and twist just a little bit at the hands of another crippling rejection - scoliosis built by sadness. I quickly catalog my life's experiences, but there is nothing floating around in my head that could possibly make her happy or make her understand.

I close my mouth and follow behind her silently. Sam sets her eyes ahead and marches on, unconcerned with the sad little dog nipping at her heels. Her boots drag across the ground, scrunching the fallen leaves. As we pass through long flat patches her steps acquire a hypnotic rhythm and the scrunching sounds take on deeper messages to my scorched psyche.

First - "*ScrooshILoveYouSam ScrooshILoveYouSam*" and then as we start up an incline - "*ThisIsHopeless ThisIsHopeless.*"

She leads us along the choked river towards the busted bridge. Yellow police tape rings the entrance where the bridge once stood. The pavement around the path is shattered into pieces that are slowly crumbling into the green muck. The bridge itself is still lying solidly in the stiff algae. We stop at the base and look over the cliff.

Sam seems completely unconcerned about returning to the scene of her crime. The twisted steel I-beams sit at odd angles beneath us. Nothing has sunk more than two or three feet. There is no machinery assembled or any other evidence that some power structure is planning on removing this mess from the river.

Sam stands over her destruction and kicks a loose piece of tar towards the tangled metal. We watch as the rock tumbles down the side of the river and *splunks* softly into the compressed muck. It sits on top of the green layer, unmoving. She picks up a bigger piece and fires it into the river. The second piece lodges itself firmly in the sludge without a bounce. An air bubble burps up, releasing another whiff of decay.

We watch downstream as a gust of wind picks up steam, moving down between the riverbeds and swiping up through the bald trees towards us. We see it coming and brace ourselves for the burst of stench that will accompany it. Sam covers her face as I puff out my chest and inhale deeply, letting the aroma hit me where it may. The green death is there but more in the background than I expected, instead, the wind smells of fire. Down the river banks a plume of smoke drifts above the tree line.

"Fire," I say to Sam, pointing toward the edge of town.

She takes another look at the old dead bridge rusting slowly beneath us. Sam seems bothered, perhaps by the lack of fuss anyone has seemingly put up in the weeks since she took it down, just letting it lie there, decomposing, without so much as a second thought from anyone even for scrap value. She boots another piece of tar and watches as it clangs off the top of the bridge and settles in the muck then shifts her gaze downriver towards the smoke.

When I saw Sam take down that bridge, there were people around - driving down the roads, milling around the town forest. Today there are no signs of activity. Only the smoke in the distance and dusty food wrappers betray that some sort of advanced species once occupied this area.

With a conscious effort, Sam breaks her scowl and shoots me a look of forced cheer. Something fundamental seems to have shifted inside her over the past few days. Her eyebrows arch over a fake smile stuck across her mouth like a sticker. The muscles in her face engage in a tug of war, pulling on the corners of her lips. She fights it for a few seconds and then gives up and lets it all collapse with a sigh, looking worriedly towards the smoke. I appreciate the show for my benefit.

"Well, we should keep moving."

The river gurgles again, belching another bubble of stench up over the bank, assaulting our nostrils, urging us to move on.

"This feels ..." I pause searching for the right word, before settling, "odd."

"Yeah," Sam breathes deeply and cringes at the smell, "but no sense in standing here all day. Right?"

"Right," I concede nervously.

She shakes her head once in agreement and starts off again towards the smoke.

"Let's go see what's happening down there."

We move a respectful distance away from the river, muting its toxic smell, and follow its winding course away from the bridge. We're close enough to town now that the road is visible through the scrawny trees. No cars or people pass by. The birds have flown south for the season and the bugs have died off. There are no sounds except for our shuffling.

The town's maintained paths are recognizable now. Sam follows them towards the smoke, unconcerned about the potential for human contact or maintaining any sort of cover. Quickly we pass out of the edge of the forest and break into the residential neighborhood where I once lay on the porch unwittingly recording Sam with my glasses. Before there were three houses standing side by side on quarter-acre lots, notable only for their decay and vandalism. Now they are the source of the smoke, leaving behind nothing but smoldering husks.

The trees around them bear the scars of the flames. Live coals glow amongst the scarce beams that remain standing on the concrete foundations. While we watch, a two by four on the farthest house crashes into the rubble sending sparks flying. The ground is dry: no one has tried to put the fires out.

The only sign anyone has cared to investigate is the original front door of the nearest house with "ABANDON HOPE" emblazoned across in neon orange letters leaning purposefully against the still-standing chimney.

Sam surveys the scene with a confused frown then looks towards the road as it winds emptily into the center of town.

"Let's go see what's going on.".

"I don't know," I say skeptically. "There is probably a good reason no one is around."

Sam considers my misgivings, then sets her jaw and pulls the notebook out of a pocket in her sweatshirt. She flips through a few pages probably looking for just the right combination of words to steel my spine and set my legs in motion. She stops flipping, marking a line with one-pointed index finger, "Emma Goldman wrote: 'People have only as much liberty as they have the intelligence to want and the courage to take." Satisfied, she closes the book and hides it back into her clothing.

"Besides," Sam adds turning her eyes back to me, "did you want to go back to camp to be with Cap?"

I shrink under her gaze and at the thought of going back and bathing in more of Cap's impotent rage.

"We'll stick along the outskirts, away from the center of town," she concedes before cutting off any further debate and moving towards the empty road. I follow, because, well ... because.

The town is split by a main street into two sides, ringed with businesses and the skeletons of old restaurants. Dozens of short, back streets break out from the center in lazy, half-formed circles. The river borders the town, set back behind a healthy layer of pine, oak, and birch forests.

Sam moves towards the edge of the cover then adjusts to follow the line of trees while watching for signs of life. We circle the town, tucked out of sight behind old dilapidated apartment buildings. Benches and streets are empty, gone are the hungry hordes milling around and no normals are left to carefully navigate the unwashed masses.

Reflexively, I reach for a missing lump underneath my shirt, missing the sensation of the glasses and their constant but comforting buzzing. My hands fall to the front pockets of my pants, confirming what I already know, my phone is gone too. Returning to familiar surroundings brings back familiar compulsions. The craving to open the LOVE app or filter through endless news items is almost debilitating in its forcefulness. The emptiness of the town feeds the compulsion too. There are no mysteries allowed in life anymore that can't be solved with a few quick flicks of a thumb.

We work our way past a cluster of buildings and get a clear view of the town square. The exploded carcass of the metal shipping container lies nakedly on the pavement. More of Sam's handiwork that no one has bothered to clean up.

Blinds are drawn on the buildings we are huddled behind, but behind them the corners of windows twinkle with the flickering light of some irrepressible screen. Life persists even in the dark.

We move away from the town square and circle the block hugging the tree line. There is still a way to go before we get to the campaign headquarters, but the strangeness of the now ghost town is distracting. There is no way to travel through it without being conspicuous.

Above us on a second level apartment, a set of curtains are open. A little face in the window stares out, chin in hands, the very epitome of boredom. From this distance the child is androgynous, and its eyes latch onto Sam like a tractor beam. I tug on Sam's shirt, stopping our progress, and point to the window. She looks up and frowns. A little hand disengages from its chin and is raised to the kid's ear level in a wave.

"Let's go," Sam hisses, not waving back.

Ignoring her command and with my neck craned up, squinting into the overcast sky, I gesture back. The kid smiles at the acknowledgment, happily shaking its hand more assertively. A happy child should be contagious, but a flood of malaise flows down from the open curtains washing over my face, rinsing me in sadness.

The curtain flutters around the child's head and its face disappears backwards into the blackness. A second face immediately takes its place at the glass. The child's mother looks out. Her eyes search down below the window anxiously. Sam grabs me by the shirt and pulls us behind the trunk of a tree, out of sight.

"What the fuck was that?" she says exasperatedly. "Something isn't right here; we need to stay out of sight."

A rebellious streak runs across my heart. This is my town and my people. Sam isn't from around here. All she knows about is being a criminal. I don't feel like being told what to do right now.

In an act of pointless but deliberate rebellion, I stick my head out from behind the tree and back towards the window. The mother's eyes meet mine immediately. Startled, I take a shaky step backward and fall to the ground. Sam swears again and scrambles to help me up.

I watch our dance reflected on the window. Behind our opaque struggling bodies, I see the woman's lips moving. Somewhere to our left sirens ring out. There is little chance the two occurrences are unrelated; such is the breathtaking efficiency of our times.

The mother's mouth closes with a snap and she stares out at both of us. I search her eyes looking for something, perhaps regret, and find nothing. The drapes close cutting off our view of her head.

The siren gets louder. Sam looks like she wants to hit me - a tiny, pink ball of fury.

I gulp and manage an "I'm sorry."

It hurts to see her looking at me like this. I feel the open sore I carry for her being cauterized with each successive failure. It was unwise to cross her.

Sam ignores the apology and finishes pulling me off the ground. "Hurry, we have to keep moving"

On our feet we follow our noses, moving away from town back towards the river. We find it again easily. All roads lead back here, so it seems.

When we run out of ground to walk, Sam turns in a huff and opens her mouth to yell at me some more. I flinch in anticipation. Confronted by my pathetic-ness, she swallows the words back, takes a deep breath, and channels some of that zen, martial arts stuff she does every morning. Composed, she says, "Have you ever seen anything like that here before?"

I shake my head.

Sam takes a deep breath in through her nose and lets it out her mouth, "I don't know what to do."

The answer seems obvious to me, we go back to the camp and forget about all of this. I don't know how to say this to her, but what little conviction I ever had has been easily shaken.

Sam's eyes flutter and her cheeks flush deep red as she thinks through the options. Watching her, my spine stiffens again, and the utility of our mission falls back into focus. All I want to do is exactly whatever it will take for her to like me. Sam sees me staring, blushes, and half-turns away, falling back into deep thought.

I take a seat on the ground facing the slime and decide to wait her out. My fingers splay out across the earth, playing with the dried leaves and twigs, unaccustomed to the clarity of thought possible with a mind unencumbered by screens. Behind me, Sam paces back and forth, deep in thought. I sit back and wait for the genius to wash over me.

Voices start to rise through the trees back from the way we came, leaves crunching loudly under their feet.

Sam spins on her heels and mouths, "Fuck." We both look around desperate for a place to hide. There are no rock outcroppings or fallen logs, just bare trees, and dead leaves. We're out in the open, exposed. Wide-eyed, Sam searches for some unseen option to present itself. She drops to her stomach then pulls me down to her level. The voices and footsteps get closer.

"There's only one option," she whispers in my ear, motioning towards the river with her eyeballs.

That doesn't seem like an option to me.

"Are you ready?" she asks.

I am *not* ready.

"On the count of three."

"One."

A dog whines back where the voices are coming from. I picture an old-fashioned search party, with mutated wolves straining against their collars, the taste of blood on their lips.

"Two."

The green river gurgles behind us. The thought of the phlegmy green algae near my mouth makes me gag.

"Three!" Sam tucks and rolls away from me.

After two full revolutions, she hits the edge of the bank and tumbles over the side like a gymnast. I watch over my shoulder and hear a faint splunk as she hits the muck.

Alone on my stomach, paralyzed by indecision, my mouth dries up. Half my muscles fight to push my flesh back towards Sam and the river, the other half fight to send me sprinting in the opposite direction. It ends in a sedentary stalemate - a huddling ball of cowardice waiting to be found. The best I can think to do is to flip over on my back and pretend that I am casually sleeping.

A dog whines behind my head and I hear a disembodied voice say, "there he is." With my eyes closed tightly, I feign sleep. Maybe they'll think I'm a left-behinder, sleeping one off. I don't hear anything from Sam down in the river. I hope she hasn't been sucked into the abyss.

"Sir! Sir! Don't move," a voice barks over my shoulder.

I close my eyes tight. The footsteps stop above my head. A dog is panting, its hot breath hitting my forehead. The animal makes a soft yelp as some unseen force pulls it back. I squint my eyes tighter, watching the fireworks display taking place underneath my eyelids.

"Sir?" a foot taps my shoulder tentatively, checking to see if they have a hobo or a dead body on their hands. I flinch at the contact. Hobo.

"Sir, can you open your eyes, please?" the voice is courteous but authoritative.

This plan is not a plan at all. There is no acceptable exit except to give up and open my eyes. I wonder if they can see Sam. I peel apart my eyelids and stare up into the gray, murky sky. What a time to be alive.

"Sir, are you injured?" the still unseen voice asks.

I shake my head "no" at the very polite ghost. Leaves and twigs stick in my hair, pinching my scalp as my head twists.

"Sir, can you go ahead and sit up, slowly? Please keep your hands visible at all times"

I scrunch up on my elbows and sit up, then swivel around on my butt. There are two cops, dressed head to toe in blue, their caps pulled down tightly over their eyes, matching blond mustaches staining their upper lips. Their uniforms have wiped away any traces of our shared humanity, drowning it in blue polyester, tight haircuts, and shoe polish.

In full regalia they look like twins, or some advertisement for Michaels' Youth. Each one holds a short leash tightly. Two beasts strain against their bondage, eager to take a piece out of me. One of the cops says something sharply in a foreign tongue and both dogs immediately come to a heel, their muzzles shiny with spittle.

"Sir, what are you doing out here?"

I consider the question. "Well, you know, just enjoying the fresh air," I stutter in reply, but quickly give away that I am not drunk.

The cops' eyes move from my ashy beard to my matted hair and filthy clothing, plainly disbelieving the words that tumble out of my mouth. They blink at me dumbly.

"Sir, you can't be out here. Can I see your ID?"

"I dropped and shattered my phone, and," I pat my pockets dramatically, "I lost my wallet."

The cops lick their lips in frustration. The dogs, perhaps sensing a change in the air, whine and paw the turf.

"What is your name?"

That is a good question and it catches me off-guard. I'm used to having an electronic aid to announce my presence. My brain comes up blank. Finally, "Jacob Trout" blurts out of my lips. That feels right.

"Sir, this area has a shelter-in-place order in effect. Where do you live?"

I can't keep track of which one of these cops is talking to me at any given moment. Staring at the two of them is dizzying.

"Umm," my vision swims and doubles, adding unnecessary redundancy to the uniforms as I struggle to remember where I used to, technically still, live. It's only been a few nights with Sam at the camp, but it already feels like a lifetime. Perhaps the fumes from the river are pickling my brain. I picture Sam slowly sinking into the green muck like a desert explorer caught in quicksand.

"Umm," I continue, rubbing my forehead to buy more time until the light dawns. "I live off of Main down by the Michaels headquarters."

The dogs lick their chops and eagerly paw at the ground. I can't tell for sure, but I think I see the cops let out a few centimeters of slack on their leashes. Below us, the river releases a thick belch, maybe from digesting Sam.

"Sir, you can't be out here."

"I know … I'm sorry. I just needed to get some air and then I fell asleep, and … umm, I didn't plan on being out here this long."

"Is there anyone else with you?"

"No," I answer a little too quickly.

"Sir, we had a report of two people including a female out here." He pauses, eyes searching my face. "You understand, I'm sure that footage of this area is not hard to find and if you were out here for a criminal purpose, we will find out, right?"

With a deep effort, I do my best to hold all the muscles in my face steady, expressionless.

"I haven't seen or heard anyone else. Should I just head back home then?" I offer hopefully.

The cops tilt their heads to the side in unison. Wry smiles tweak the edges of their mouths. Looking at each other, they pass some telepathic communication back and forth through shared wiring.

"Sir, don't move. We are going over there to talk, and we'll be right back, understand?"

With their thick mustaches covering their upper lips, I have trouble tracking which one the words are coming out of. The cop on one side points to a patch of underbrush about fifty feet behind them.

I nod and the other one ties off one of the wolves to a tree right beside me. The beast watches as its master walks away then turns and stares through me. The skin around its lips twitch spastically, and muscles ripple across its legs while it sits delicately on its haunches waiting for an excuse to taste human flesh.

I rock forward adjusting my weight and instantly the dog comes to attention, snarling. One of the cops turns around to see what is going on. I fall back on my butt and the cop turns his back as the dog eases off.

I imagine part of the animal's training must include merciless, spirit breaking beatings by people dressed like mud puddles. Pounding a hot lust for hobo blood into the creatures is the only way to keep the peace around here. I decide not to test the strength of the leash or the sapling it is tied to.

I can't hear what the cops are saying. I try to read lips as their mustaches bounce up and down. I think I see one of them mouth the word "whore" or "poor". Whore would make more sense. Why else would some dummy risk running around in the woods if not to get his rocks off? One pulls out a screen and runs his fingers across the interface.

Still no sign of Sam from over the embankment.

Both the cops study the results on their screen and shake their head in unison, coming to an apparent consensus before they stomp back over in their gleaming boots. The dog never takes its murderous eyes off me while the leash is untied from the tree.

"Sir, we're going to escort you back home. There are a few bands of rioters still unaccounted for. It's not safe to be out here. The shelter-in-place order is going to extend at least through the night."

Relief passes over me as a smile tugs at the corners of my mouth, I fight back against the muscles, not wanting to give too much away. It hadn't occurred to me there could be a way out of this whole mess. Without Sam in clear view, the spell she holds is muted.

At this moment I yearn for no greater purpose than Go-Bars, hot showers, video games, and another stupid job. Sam and Cap can go back to wherever they came from and the consequences of this whole thing will just wash off me.

The silence around us is broken by a low whirring sound. Two hovering black discs emerge at the top of the tree line and pause. They're combat drones, like the ones I use in DRONE. I've never seen one in real life before or against a landscape that wasn't a desert. Gray light glints off the lens of the camera mounted in their centers. These two look like they still have their full payload.

Behind a screen, someone is staring down at us. Menace radiates off the machines. I feel naked traipsing around out here in real life, playing the big bad terrorist.

"What the fuck? I thought this area was clear." The cops have noticed our company.

Reaching down in unison they each put a hand under my armpits and set me up on my feet. The dogs' sense of disappointment is palpable as they realize no order to kill is forthcoming.

"We need to get to cover. Where is the girl?"

"What girl?" I reply dumbly. "What is going on?"

A frustrated sigh escapes under the mustache of the one on my left. "A clan of renegade players hacked the system and laid down a patch allowing anyone to joyride the drones. It seems to have coordinated with the riots. We've cleaned up most of them, but apparently there is still some work to do. God only knows how they got them all the way over here." They un-holster their guns, as the drones hover in front of us.

I can tell we aren't in the kill zone yet. If either one of these cops is a half-decent shot, then the operators are at a disadvantage now that we've spotted them. They don't have adequate cover to get overhead.

I learned a long time ago not to take on an armed target face-to-face. These models can't launch rockets or other cool projectiles. All they can do is drop cluster bombs. It is for this reason that the element of surprise is key.

Without turning, the cops pull me backward away from the river. The one on the right speaks into an unseen transmitter in his cuff. "We've got two more in the park. Full armed. We're prepared to engage." He sights his pistol on the horizon and speaks to his partner. "I'm going to take these two out. You watch him."

The cop drags me away as his partner drops into a shooting stance. The drones buzz and begin some simple evasive maneuvers. Whoever is piloting them can't be any higher than red squadron. I passed that skill-level months ago. The drones separate and swoop in unsteadily towards us.

The cop moves like lightening, cracking off two bullets so quickly I can hardly distinguish the sound between the shots. The drones pause their flight patterns and hover for a second before dropping out of the air in unison. Satisfied, he holsters his gun and turns back towards us.

"We'll have to get a munitions crew in here to clean that up," he says to his partner. "Sir, as you can see it still isn't safe out here. We confirmed your address in the system, and we are going to follow you back to the building. Under no circumstances, absent a medical emergency are you to be back out here. Do you understand?"

"Understood," I confirm.

I wonder if Sam drowned. I doubt the river ever gives up its dead. If a drone had found her first, we would have heard the bomb it dropped.

One of the cops steps in front of me, his dog heeled tightly at his side. The other falls in line behind me and together we march the rest of the way across town to the door of my apartment building. I see the curtains in the first-floor ruffle at our approach and then close tightly.

I put my hand on the knob and mercifully it turns. I turn and smile at the two cops and their dogs like an idiot. They nod their heads and I take the stairs up to the second floor. It feels like I am closing a chapter. My apartment door is unlocked, and I swing it open in relief.

The door shuts behind me with a click. The air is musty and stale from the laundry still strewn across the floor. I stride across the kitchen towards the bedroom, dropping more articles of clothing as I go. Peeling the last layer of underwear off as I make it to the bathroom.

I crank the handle of the faucet in the shower all the way to the left. Steam immediately begins filling the air and my lungs. Stepping into the stall, the water scalds my skin, boiling away layers of grime and regret. I peel off a nub of soap melted to the side of the stall and scrub at the outer layer of skin.

A pressure valve in my head releases and under the steamy water, safely ensconced back in the cocoon of my crappy little apartment full of my numbing little distractions, a laugh starts deep in my stomach, ripping through my innards before spraying out of my mouth in uncontrollable waves.

The reaction is irresistible, so I slouch down in the shower and give in, letting the euphoria wash over me like the water. It seems inconceivable now I would have ever let myself get dragged into that mess.

The water in the spout starts to sputter. There must be a restriction in place. I close the valve with my foot and sit back in the steamy room, filling my lungs. Freedom in the woods never felt as free as my guarded little life here. I still have money in my account. As soon as the shelter-in-place order is lifted, I can go get a replacement for my glasses and then find a new job.

I take another deep breath of the warm, damp air as the stress continues to melt away. My muscles relax while my brain downshifts out of survival mode. This is my place. This is where I belong.

The door connecting the kitchen to the outside hallway opens then closes with a slam. My body hardens as my over-worked adrenal glands kick in again. Footsteps make their way carefully across the apartment floor to the entrance of the bathroom.

My imagination runs wild.

Scavengers or the rioters the cops were talking about have come to steal whatever little scraps they can find. I wonder how far away the twin cops are, and how shrill I would have to be for them to hear me scream. Whoever has broken in is now casting a shadow underneath the bottom of the door.

"Who's there?" I yell into the unknown, my voice quaking. "There are some Go-Bars in the pantry. Just take them and leave. I don't have anything else."

The shadow feet stand there considering the offer. Does it have a taste for blood or vacuum packed, condensed nutrition particles? Choosing blood, the doorknob turns swinging the door open. I pick the only rational self-defense option left and grab my withering penis with both hands, clutching it in fear.

Sam stands in the open doorway, staring into the note-book open in her hand. Her clothes are grimy, and she reeks of vegetable death, her face streaked with dirt. Clearing her throat, she reads, "The first lesson a revolutionary must learn is that he is a doomed man - Huey Newton."

Seeing her standing there is the most terrifying of all the options my brain had been able to conjure.

"Do you know who Huey Newton was?" she asks, dropping the notebook on the floor and stripping off her crud covered sweatshirt.

Casually, she pulls her bra over her head and turns straight towards me. I can feel my eyes widen to the size of saucer plates. She pulls down her pants and underwear in one swoop and makes a motion for me to move over. Hands still cupped over my crotch, I scoot back as best as possible and Sam climbs into the shower in front of me. She pulls the faucet handle towards her and the water sputters out, weak at first as air works out of the pipes, then stronger.

It trickles down her shoulders in thick rivulets, pooling at the small of her back and flowing off her butt like a waterfall. She pulls the remainder of the soap from the tray, works up a lather with both hands then runs it through her hair. Sam doesn't stand much more than five feet tall, but she looks like a giant towering over me, naked in the tub.

"Well?" Sam asks with both hands above her shoulders rubbing the soap out of her hair. My jaw hangs open, stupidly.

"Well, what?" I manage, surprised my brain is able to contribute any words at all.

Sam laughs and turns towards me, full-frontal, leaning her head back into the faucet. "Well, do you know who Huey Newton was?" she replies.

The circuit board overloads, tripping every breaker on the way out. All I can do it shake my head "no".

Sam laughs again, "Huey Newton was Martin Luther King Jr.'s dry cleaner and bodyguard. He founded the Black Panthers with Malcolm X. You should read some of his treatises, they are so inspirational." The water runs out again and Sam twists the knobs off.

She looks down at me, holding my eye contact. Transfixed I stare up at her and warm water starts suddenly running all over my legs. Startled, I look down as Sam unleashes a torrent of urine all over my lower half. I look up aghast. Her eyes are burning with rage.

"Listen you motherfucker. If you ever leave me alone again … if you ever disobey another order I give you, I will fucking kill you. The time to run away is over. Do you understand? You had your chance. Now you are committed to this, to see this through. There is no turning back. Understand?" With obvious effort, she clenches something inside herself and the pee stops abruptly.

"Jake, do you understand?" The skin on her face is pulled back in a smooth mask and her eyes are wide. Looking into them is a horror I can't stomach. "I want to hear an answer. A real answer. Do you understand?"

"I understand," I manage meekly.

"Good. Now, do you mind?" she asks.

My heads swirls, "What?" I manage.

Sam shakes her head in exaggerated exasperation, "I have to pee really bad. Do you mind moving? Unless you want me to go all over your legs?" Her mood has shifted and she seems playful again, almost jovial.

Sam flicks her head towards the door, "Give me a couple of minutes."

I mumble something and scurry out from underneath her and grab a towel from the hanger. I rub it over my legs, trying to scrub them clean.

"We can hang out here for a little bit, at least until nightfall, then we'll head back to camp. I don't want to leave Cap alone for too long," her voice leaks out around the shower curtain over the splatter of urine. It is clear I have sorely misjudged this animal in my shower.

She finishes and a disembodied hand reaches out from the shower groping blindly at the towel rod. I don't know why I'm still standing here. Sometimes prisons are our own constructs and sometimes they have pink hair.

I escape out the door into my bedroom and quickly rustle up some clean clothes. The bathroom door opens and closes then Sam is standing in my bedroom with a towel wrapped around her. Even though I heard her coming, I still jump a little when I see her.

"Can I borrow some clothes?" she asks.

I root through my closet and emerge with a t-shirt, some oversized sweatpants, and a pair of clean socks. She drops the towel and delicately steps into the pants. I turn my back, face burning bright red. She cinches the pants around her waist and disappears back into the living room, where I find her nestled on the couch reading from her notebook. I stand in the doorway watching her exist in my space. Eventually, she closes the notebook and cracks the curtain along the front bay window to look out.

"I think I can just make out the top of the headquarters from here," she comments, straining her neck to look up the street. "This reconnaissance of ours didn't really turn out the way we thought it would, huh?"

Things rarely do.

CHAPTER ELEVEN

Dreams

Sam is asleep curled into a tight ball on the couch. I don't know what to do with her.

My neck hurts. We spent the night watching TV. I have no idea what we watched, only that it succeeded in switching my brain off, enabling me to drift off to sleep on the chair in the living room. It's still on, blabbering away in the corner.

Sam's chest rises and falls slowly. A spot of drool winds its way down her chin. This is the first time I have ever caught sight of her sleeping. Usually, she is up with the sun doing her yoga or kung fu or whatever.

There is a pillow on the floor beneath her. She looks so small and helpless sleeping on my couch. I could pick up the pillow and smother her face with it. I'm fairly certain that with my full body weight pressing down on her, I would be able to suffocate her. Staring at the pillow, I let the scenario play out over and over again in my head. I could pin her arms down with my legs and lean into it. It would be over before she knew what happened. I could be free.

Sam stirs and mutters something in her sleep, breaking the spell. There is no such thing as freedom anymore.

I make my way to the cupboard and rustle up a half-empty box of Go - Bars. Sam's eyes flutter open as I tear apart the wrapper.

"Want one?" I offer.

Through a yawn and stretch, she shakes her head "no." Somehow the bar is worse even than the wretched produce I stared down death for.

The light reflecting off the TV changes suddenly as the talking face on the screen is minimized and moved to the top corner. Text fills the screen: SHELTER-IN-PLACE LIFTED - DAYLIGHT CURFEW IN EFFECT UNTIL FURTHER NOTICE.

Sam nods at the set, "Looks like our little vacation is coming to an end."

A chunk of Go-Bar lodges itself in my throat. The pressure starts building up behind my eyes again at the thought of re-entering Sam's world and completing the tasks required to keep me alive. Bricks of resistance are laid as my body, for the first time in its wretched life, prepares to fight back.

Sam completes her stretch with a pop and moves into the bathroom, seating herself firmly on the toilet without bothering to close the door. These are life's perks, I guess. With her elbows on her knees, she begins flipping through her notebook. I turn my back and move out of view of the doorway.

Sam reads aloud, "The greatest mistake of the move-ment has been trying to organize a sleeping people around specific goals. You have to wake the people up first, then you'll get action. - Malcolm X." There is a pause and then the toilet flushes.

She emerges from the bathroom holding her soiled clothes in a trash bag. "Are you ready to go?"

I gulp down the rest of my breakfast and consider her question. It isn't really a question. It's a statement that tried on a question's clothes and went out dancing. Her mood again is light, making no hint at her performance in the shower last night. I shrug my shoulders and look around the apartment for something to distract myself with. A pair of dirty cups on the table catches my eye and I bring them over to the sink.

"Well, we can't stay here much longer. We have to com-plete the recon on the target and then get back to camp before sundown. It'll be tough to travel once the curfew is up," she continues.

I nod in agreement at whatever she is saying. With the dishes clean, I look around for something else to wash. There is nothing else in my Spartan lifestyle that requires immediate attention.

Reluctantly, I turn around. Sam smiles and cinches the drawstring on my borrowed pants tighter. Any resistance or murder I may have mounted has melted away. Somehow going with her to follow through on our wretched plans is the coward's way out. It has all the hallmarks of courage, but I know better.

"Yeah, one second, alright?" I beg.

Smiling falsely, I make my way into my bedroom and slowly change my clothes again. Then I move into the bathroom, close the door, and pretend to crap. There is nothing inside me to expel but I keep up the charade for as long as I can.

Sam knocks on the door, "Are you OK?"

"Fine," I yell back, lying as the water flushes down the pipes.

I look around the room bug-eyed for something else to stall with. All I can find is a toothbrush with no paste. I pick it up and stare into the mirror, rubbing it slowly in a circular motion across my gums, begging for some heroic brain cell to compose a coherent plan.

I should lock the door and tell her to leave, then wait it out in here. The best place to survive an apocalypse is in the bathroom. There is light and water, and a place to shit. Eating toothpaste, I'm sure I could last alone in here for days, maybe weeks. Saliva starts leaking out around the toothbrush. A plan starts to formulate but step one fails: the door to the bathroom doesn't lock.

Damnit.

I pull in closer to the mirror and take a deep look at my teeth, plaque is built up in solid columns, filling all the cracks with yellow mortar. I better floss. Doubling up the string between my fingers, I meticulously excavate between each tooth. I complete the cycle three times until my spittle is tinted red, flecked with blood.

Sam raps impatiently on the door with a knuckle. "Are you coming out?"

Standing in front of the mirror, gums bleeding, the floss hangs out, trapped in the tight space between my front teeth.

That's a good question. I pull the floss out with a snap as the door swings open.

Sam leans against the frame staring at me with her trademark look of tired exasperation, "Your teeth look plenty clean. Can we get moving, please? We are running out of time."

A shiver runs through my body, popping up gooseflesh along my arms and neck. There are no holes in here suitable for crawling in to. "Alright," I concede.

"Great!" Sam perks up, moving off the frame. Her threat from last night runs through my head and I shudder again. Her falseness now is chilling.

Sam checks behind her to make sure I'm still following as she leads us out the front door. I turn off all the lights as we go, letting my eyes linger one last time on my comfortable cocoon. My video games sit in the corner underneath the TV, pulsing with desire, longing to be touched again. I take one more look and then follow Sam out into the hallway and down the stairs out onto the street.

The sun shines brightly, and people have started poking their heads outside, emerging from their holes, squinting. I follow Sam up the hill.

Very quickly the street feels like it is bustling. Buildings bear the scars of the run-away drones and whatever rioting the cops were talking about. A sense of optimism hangs in the air like it's the first warm day of spring. We quickly reach the top of the hill, and Sam walks up towards the building at the center of our plans - my *raisin d'être*, or whatever.

The hologram pops out to meet us, eyes wild, grin wide and devilish, eager to digitally convert any unbelievers. I jump back, startled by both the suddenness and manic look. Without my glasses as a shield, the eight-foot-tall Mike Michaels is different than the last time I stumbled into his range. His digital synapses seem frayed. Fuzzy cords stand out striated along his neck as a tiny tongue darts out of his mouth, wetting his imaginary lips.

As we stand there, his sensors digest us, cataloging our profiles for use in some undoubtedly sinister database. There's a hiccup in the feed as the machinery tries to regain self-control, scanning us, searching for glasses or a phone to connect with. The hologram seems frustrated with our inability to speak its digital language. No matter how much it tills the soil, our digital farmland is barren.

Huddled together on the sidewalk, I feel naked and exposed. Sam doesn't seem to think twice standing openly in front of the building we are planning to destroy. With her arms crossed, a bemused look spreads across her lips. Sam takes her book out from her pack and begins flipping through the pages. "It is better to live on your knees than die on your feet - Emiliano Zapata," she recites defiantly to the towering phantom. I don't know if she got the quote backward on purpose. In any case, it makes more sense to me this way.

The sidewalk has started to fill up. People filter by, taking expert care to ignore us while stepping expertly just outside the range of Mike's sensors.

Still, Mike grins emptily at us, happy to have found some willing voters, even ones neutered of his preferred means of virtual communication.

"Greetings fellow citizens! In just a few short weeks you will be asked to make a decision which will have a ripple effect on the present and future of our great nation! Cast your ballot for me - Mike Michaels! Together we can..." The hologram flickers and we lose the last and presumably best part of his pitch.

Somewhere a computer chip re-calibrates, and Mike solidifies again. His operating system apparently unaware of its glitch doesn't repeat the clinching line.

Sam stands underneath the phantom, one hand holding up my too-big pants, unintimidated by whatever devices are currently scanning and recording her. Her nose crinkles as she sniffs the air, "It smells like something is burning."

She's right. The old brick building in front of us stands three stories tall. Four large bay windows face the street on each level, all ringed in white trim. I can see at least four cameras tracking us as Sam's pink hair shines in the sun. Considering she has managed to avoid jail; I should probably trust her expertise.

Maybe the bomb Cap is making is big enough to destroy all the evidence, including the server farms where all this is being stored. Thinking about it makes me cringe and I try to obscure my face in the collar of my shirt. Everything is terrible.

The hologram shudders spastically as it resets itself. "Greetings fellow citizens..." it bellows out again from unseen speakers. Sam spits on the ground defiantly. I don't know who this little pink person is or how she came to control my life.

"Let's see what its guts look like," she decides. "I want to see inside."

I pretend to wipe my eyebrow with my shirt and turn away from the building. Maybe if I keep my face in constant motion, they won't be able to make it out. Maybe no one will think to ever run this video back. Maybe there is a way this doesn't end in disaster. Maybe the sky will fall on my head.

A glass entrance stands out against the brick facade. Sam walks through the hologram and pushes her face up against the door. She presses her nose to the glass, ringing her eyes with her hands, trying to block out the reflections to get a look inside. Behind her, I prance nervously from one foot to the other. Sam's head jerks back as the door suddenly opens by itself along a sideways track.

She looks back at me. I continue hopping back and forth like a little kid waiting for the bathroom. Sam raises her eyebrows and disappears inside. I feel like a parakeet with the door to his cage finally left ajar - freedom, sweet horrible freedom. Like a bird, I follow my reflection towards the glass on the door and peer inside to find out what Sam fell into. The sun is directly behind me and I can't make out anything inside, all I can see is a picture of my own dumb face biting down on my lower lip so hard a deep purple is beginning to pool underneath the skin.

A "whoosh" is followed by a tinny mechanical grinding sound as the door slides open again. My mouth floods with a briny, copper taste when a canine finally punctures the skin on my lip – sweet, horrible freedom. I lick the blood and cross the threshold. The door shuts behind me with a matching "swoosh".

Sam stands to one side of the threshold, looking down the hallway in front of us with her head cocked sideways. A plain receptionists' desk sits in front of us, blanketed in gaudy campaign posters featuring a stylized headshot of Mike - his eyes teeming with the same madness as the hologram outside. A stack of stickers has fallen off the desk and lies scattered across the floor.

"Do you think this is load-bearing?" Sam asks, fingering the wall delicately, like a carpenter admiring her handiwork.

She raps it lightly with two knuckles. It doesn't sound hollow. I open my mouth to say something smart, then acknowledge the enormity of that task and let it close slowly.

Along the ceiling a camera is perched in the corner, a red light blinking its greeting at us. We wait there silently in front of the door for someone to notice our presence. Outside, I can faintly hear Hologram Mike as he pops back to life, trying to deal out a heart attack to the unaware.

Sam looks up at me and shrugs. She studies my face with an ear pointed down the hallway listening for footfalls. I avoid her eye contact. There is no sign of human life anywhere.

"Let's take a look around," she suggests, causing me to visibly recoil. Seeing that I need another helping of motivation, she reaches inside herself and pulls out the beat-up notebook, flipping through until she stops on a page with her thumb.

"Ahh, here we go: 'We have it in our power to begin the world over again.' I love that one."

I don't know what that quote means, but if its intention is to get me to walk down that hall, it is both overkill and ineffective. My feet grow roots, planting me firmly where I stand.

"Ready?" Sam asks, her voice rising delicately.

I try to study the posters on the desk - memorizing the details on the red, white, and blue fonts ringing Mike's glowing head, the airbrushed alien smoothness of his forehead, the impeccable, almost plastic part in his hair. The ... Sam's face crosses into my sightline, she smiles patiently and repeats, "Ready?"

The lights flick on down the hallway automatically as she moves within range of their motion sensors. Reaching the end of the road she takes a sharp turn and disappears.

Standing alone in the foyer, the hair on my neck stands on end. Outside, Hologram Mike hollers maniacally at a new passerby. I don't want to go back out there either.

Sam lives in the woods with no discernible skills except for exploding old things and charming young idiots. I have an apartment filled with stuff I bought because someone saw fit to pay me for my time. By most measures, I am living the more successful and enriched life. But it feels like I have stepped off some precipice into a void filled only with scary thoughts and pink hair. There are no tools in my box suitable for attending to the many tasks required to build back up the cocoon of my existence. My stomach drops.

Around the corner, Sam's footfalls grow fainter.

The world spins, inching imperceptibly forward, taking all of us - walking, talking, eating, shitting, lusting, fucking - meat passengers along for the ride. The momentum nudges me in the back, breaking my death grip on the floor, and I take off down the hall at a run to catch up with Sam. I find her just around the first corner, sticking her head into an open doorway.

"Shhh," she scolds as I race towards her. "They're sleeping ... I think."

I stick my head above hers and gaze into the room. Light from the hallway illuminates the first five feet but the rest is pitch black, and it takes a second for my eyes to adjust to the din. The room seems to stretch forever. Even as I strain against the blackness, I can't see the back wall.

Sam pulls gently on my shirt and nods to one side. My pupils dilate, letting more light stream across my corneas. There are rows of beds, tucked in neat rows of five starting at the center of the room and running back to the wall. Each bed is the same, twin mattress perched atop a plain metal frame, white sheets cascading neatly off the sides. Underneath each sheet is a lump. Each lump is differently shaped but all of them rise and fall in unison.

I pull away from the door, stepping backward into the hallway, and pull on Sam's arm, "Let's get out of here." Sam rips her limb from my grip and takes another step forward.

"Not yet," she hisses, "Look."

I pause but then follow her forward into the room.

"The light is ruining my vision," she swings the door carefully back into place, leaving it unlatched, so only a sliver of light from the hall can knife its way into the darkness.

I grab her hand sending a rush of nausea through me, a traitor to myself. I fight through the queasiness and we stand there in the middle of the rows of beds, waiting to see whatever there is to see. The lumps keep rising and falling rhythmically. Atop each package are two small orbs, lit up and pointed towards the ceiling. Patterns of light pulse quickly across them, coordinated with each set on each lumpy mass.

It quickly becomes clear that the lumps are nothing more than bags of skin filled with bones and blood and stuff. The orbs fit neatly across each of the lumps' eyes, feeding who-knows-what into their nerve centers, deciding what each of the poor souls is supposed to do, say, and think.

Sam and I stand frozen in awe, watching as the lights play off the sleeping faces, flashing up and down the countless rows of bodies, like a display of Christmas lights.

"What the fuck?" Sam utters in a mixture of horror and amazement.

Throughout the room, the glasses stop blinking and turn red. A buzzing starts in the back and crashes down towards us like a wave. I hold a hand up to my face, recalling the familiar sound, remembering the feeling of them when they would vibrate, faintly tickling the bridge of my nose. Slowly, the lumps stir. We watch as starting from the back of the room, the lump on each bed sits up.

I squeeze Sam's hand hard, "Let's go."

She squeezes back and I pull her stumbling towards the door. My heel bumps into it and we jump at the sound of the lock fitting snuggly into the jamb with a loud click. Hysteria immediately drenches all the sensitive parts of my body in a thick sweat.

Dozens of glowing lenses turn in unison and face us as I stumble for the doorknob. Footsteps ring out from the hallway outside. Someone is yelling but my brain is too foggy to make sense of the words. In the slice of light, I see Sam reaching for a switch on the wall. At this moment, there is nothing in the world I want less than for her to turn on that light.

I would rather have a brain-eating parasite placed up my nose with tweezers made of used razor blades.

I would rather have my scalp torn off my skull by a baboon I had raised as my own child for years.

The universe decides for me, reinforcing that my opinions are completely irrelevant. Sam flicks the switch on flooding us with violent neon light. It burns my eyes and I squint.

The lines of white beds run all the way back to the wall. There is a staggering amount of humanity contained in this room. With the lights on, my brain begins to fully process the scene - the sheer mustiness of so many people breathing and farting in such proximity is overwhelming.

Three beds are close enough to the door that Sam and I could reach out and touch their plain white sheets. Three girls, or women, sit up and stare at us through the pulsing glass covering their eyes. I think I recognize the middle one, maybe from the LOVE app. They stare at us confused but devoid of anger. Their motions coordinated puppetry, smooth and slow, rendered into a dreamlike quality. Their heads tilt to the side then rotate backward in a slow circle as if working out a kink in their necks. Their expressions are peaceful, but I can't feel anything except profound sadness.

All at once, the light drains from their glasses. Throughout the room, the little pulsing dots blink once more and then clear. In front of us, the women's eyes uncluttered by whatever was being pumped into their brains, refocus, and settle on me, really seeing us for the first time. They pause, eyes widening, muscles tensing, sucking in air deeply through flared nostrils before pushing it out violently across their vocal cords in a prolonged scream of pure terror. It starts in the front of the room but quickly migrates throughout - a synchronized chorus of shrieking, drowning out all other sounds.

Gooseflesh breaks out across my arms and legs as my heart speeds up into an unsustainable panic. Refusing to participate any further my brain checks out sending me to claw blindly for the exit. Sam finds the handle and pulls the door open, pouring us back out into the hallway in a damp panic. I trip over my feet and sprawl across the floor on my back, panting like a dog locked in a car in July. Sam shuts the door behind us muting the screams.

I think a little bit of pee squeezes out of my urethra.

I think a high-pitched squealing is also pouring out of my mouth.

"Who are you? You can't be in there. This is private property." At a half run, a man with stark white eyebrows and no hair approaches us from down the hallway.

I push my back against the wall and do my best to stop the squeaking sound escaping from my lungs. He looks down at me and his chin visibly recoils.

"What are you doing here?" he demands, ignoring the muffled screams taking place behind the closed door, "The interns are sleeping."

Sam steps between us, "We waited but there was no one at the front desk." Her voice is friendly but elevated, struggling to be heard over the din coming from the interns.

"Fucking Cassandra! I told her never to leave the front desk uncovered. We can't have this," he says to himself. "The interns are sleeping. They work long shifts and it is very important they have an opportunity to recharge. They had just entered their meditative state and you broke the cycle on their apps. There is important work being done here." He opens a console in the wall and types furiously. After a moment the screams behind the door quiet down.

Conveniently, my lungs run out of oxygen and the mortifying sounds stop falling out of my mouth. I quickly pull myself up along the wall and stand behind Sam, gasping like a hooked fish flapping around on the deck of a boat.

The man looks at us incredulously. "Well..."

"What?"

"Go on, you have to leave. I said you can't be back here. This is private property. You aren't allowed in here." He makes a shooing motion with his hands and begins herding us back from where we came. Sam pauses to say something else then thinks better of it and allows us to be rounded up. We make the long walk back to the waiting area in silence.

He stops at the desk, standing between us and the hallway with his arms crossed. "What did you want, anyway?" He makes a concerted effort to soften his tone and pretend everything is normal. His eyes, darting around nervously, betray him.

Sam and I look at each other, caught flatfooted by the obvious question, and unsure of what lies to tell. "To volunteer," Sam finally blurts out.

He studies us up and down, mouth twisted into a tight 'O.' "We appreciate the enthusiasm. It is only through the dedication of supporters like you that Mike will be able to cut through all the lies in the media and win this November." He recites as he turns and picks two large stacks of flyers and stickers off the desk and hands them to Sam. She takes them, passing the stickers to me.

"Have a good day," he says with finality, powder-white eyebrows rising in a fine arch.

The door slides open behind us and we stumble out onto the sidewalk. The hologram instantly springs to life again. Sam ignores its pleadings and quickly moves out of the range of his electronic eye.

"That was some weird shit." She is barely able to conceal the excitement in her voice.

"It sort of makes sense. Have you ever used one of the meditation apps?" I counter.

Sam looks at me aghast and shakes her head "no."

"They're a great way to turn your brain off. Lots of people use them as sleep aids," I add with all the confidence I can muster.

I realize this seems like I have an endless appetite for bullshit rationalization, but I don't want to explode this building anymore. I'm not sure if I ever did. Sam is right, of course, that was a bunch of weird fucked-up shit. I feel obligated to play dumb, refusing to help build her case.

Good poker players hide their cards. Bad poker players scream in fright and wet their underwear. Sam stares back at me incredulous at my density.

"Sam, there are people in there. We can't do this," I plead.

"Those aren't people. They're something else." Sam sets her jaw quizzically then without another word moves off down the sidewalk.

I take a running first step to catch up with her. The streets are filling up with people. It feels like the entire town is collectively stretching its legs. Sam parts the crowds quickly, brazenly. I wallow behind her, pulled along by the suction of her wake.

She chooses to follow the main streets straight out of town, no skirting along the alleyways and park lanes. A second shift of interns in white shirts stands at every corner passing out flyers with a picture of Michaels grinning and "VOTE" emblazoned across the top in dark red letters.

His face covers the ground as people discard the flyers as fast as they are foisted into their hands. Mike's eyes don't look as dead on paper as they do in hologram.

The milling crowd is mixed, some workers hide behind their glasses, while the left-behinders are open and exposed. The programming inside my brain releases the precise recipe of chemicals flooding me with regret and melancholy. I touch under my eyes compulsively, feeling for the glasses like a lost limb. The world somehow feels bigger, scarier, less digestible without the constant reminders of the acceptable human reactions and priorities the glasses provided. The bad chemicals flood my senses hard enough to make me squint.

We approach a group of women my age, all of them wearing their glasses. An overwhelming urge to access the LOVE app shudders through my bones. We pass undetected in front of their uninterested screens.

I am adrift, lost between two worlds.

Sam's pink hair bobs in front of me - the only life raft in a sea of confusion. We pass a tangled mass of steel, former ration station, current modern art exhibit, or criminal act of social commentary. I'm not sure. Either way, Sam doesn't stop to admire her past handiwork. She picks up the pace. I jog to keep pace.

The sweet smell of a cigar tickles my nostrils as we approach a set of benches in the middle of the square. Sam heads between them. The two guys who bullied me for my ration box and later robbed me of my dignity are there sitting together, puffing on their grape-flavored cigars, and enjoying the outside. Blindly following Sam quickly leads me into their orbit.

We are blocked in by the sea of people. There is no escape sideways or backward. I pull closer to her like a little kid holding onto his mom's skirt and hope that they won't notice.

Sam moves around a slow couple, jumping suddenly down off the sidewalk, and I can't keep up with her zig. Alone and exposed I lock eyes with the shorter one. He elbows the taller one in the ribs and nods towards me. They grin in unison chewing and puffing on the ends of their stumpy cigars. Their faces are bleary and their eyes dull. They must have sheltered in place inside a bottle.

"Look who it is!" the tall one says, standing up towards me.

"Hey there Rich Boy, you sure look like ten pounds of shit. What's going on?" his friend adds.

The commotion on the street quiets down as people stop to watch. A sense of déjà vu washes over me. Instinctually, I grab hold of the waist on my pants and look for an exit. My mouth turns dry which is fine because my brain can't formulate a proper response anyway. The fight or flight response buried deep within my nervous system decides on a third, less celebrated, but equally alliterative option – I freeze. I grope for Sam, but she's disappeared down the street.

They circle me like a pair of wolves, eager to impress the growing crowd with another public bullying.

"Where you been? Off picking on other helpless old men?" the tall one taunts, turning to the onlookers, establishing I deserve whatever is coming at me.

"No," I fumble stupidly to laughter from the group.

The two of them grin, happy to find a more willing audience than the last time. The short one moves into my personal space and jabs me in the shoulder with two pointed fingers. His hot, boozy breath hits me in the chin and fills my nose.

"No?!?" he repeats, mocking my shaky voice.

I don't think we sound alike at all.

The tall one clogs one nostril with his middle finger and fires a rocket of snot out the other side. He laughs at his partner's parroting. They float around me, elated by their good fortune: the stupid fly has fallen, fully tangled, into their web again.

I've never hit anyone. The notion of resorting to physical violence is foreign, which considering the things Sam has planned for me is ironic now, I guess. It still seems more barbaric to put your hands on someone, like the difference between killing a pig and eating bacon.

This world is not for me.

My bone bag begins battening down the hatches for the bad things that are about to happen. Searching for a happy thought to camp out inside, my brain turns up the residue of a house on a lake and fishing for brook trout. I don't recognize any of the people on the boat - this must be a scene from a movie I saw as a kid. Oh well, it'll have to do. I pick up a rod, toss the line into the water and wait for a tug or gut punch or nose reconstruction or wet willy or whatever. Somewhere in front of my eyes but beyond where I can see, I hear them laugh again.

A hand grabs my arm - I reel the line in. The bait is undisturbed, but the hook has dragged in a small piece of pondweed.

The hand moves to my shoulder and begins shaking - I pull the rod back over my shoulder and cast it deep into the center of the pond. The man sitting by the outboard smiles slightly and nods his approval. He has a beautiful mustache. I think I've seen him on a billboard endorsing deodorant.

Outside people begin a heated discussion about things I no longer care about - the tip of the rod jumps once, then again, the line begins pulling out of the reel as the fish makes its run.

Someone bumps into my body; it loses its balance for a second and then recovers - I reset the drag and start reeling the fish in towards the bow of the boat. The man with the beautiful mustache readies a large green net.

A small hand slaps across my face, then grabs my cheeks between its thumb and forefinger, puckering my mouth like the fish on the line. My brain screams at my eyes not to let the light in, but they insist.

The brook trout in the net retreats. The smiling man with the mustache fades, and Sam stands in front of me with her hair blazing. My tormentors writhe on the ground in front of us, hands grasped tightly between their legs. It looks like one of them has thrown up. The short one sputters and releases a small stream of something out of the side of his mouth - solving that minor mystery.

"Jake, wake up. Let's go."

"What did you do?"

"I kicked them in the balls. Like really hard. They're down now but it won't last forever. Let's go." She has the same look on her face as she did in the shower at my apartment.

I should feel thankful, but instead, this is just a reminder - there is no way out.

Sam grabs my hand and pulls me through the crowd. People stare at us and open their mouths to protest but think better of it and part. We move quickly down the sidewalk away from the commotion. I look over my shoulder after we make it three blocks and the rabble of unwashed humanity has dispersed to mind their own business. Two bodies lie shuddering on the pavement, flopping around like fish slowing dying on the bottom of my boat.

CHAPTER TWELVE

Fucking Rockets

ollowing the banks of the constipated river, we walk the rest of the way back to the campsite without incident. I'm growing accustomed to the stench.

The days are short, and the sun sets quickly. The air bites cold as dusk settles across the woods. I tag along blindly behind Sam, unaware of our surroundings or the mysterious paths she follows. Nothing along the route looks familiar. We scale another hill and look down into a ravine. There Cap tends a small fire; smoke fills the air in the space above his head and then dissipates. I can see Cap chewing the end of a cigar and spitting it into the flames.

Sam stops us on the crest of the hill and watches as Cap stomps around the campground. He disappears into the shack and emerges with a plastic jug of water. Leaning against the doorway, Cap raises the jug to his lips and takes a long pull, his eyes never leaving the popping fire.

"Y'all going to stay up there all night, or what?" he bellows into the encroaching blackness.

Sam sighs but doesn't move from her post.

"Fuck it then," Cap grumbles returning his attention to the campfire. Shadows cast off by the flames play against his face, arching darkly over his eyebrows, up his forehead, making it look like horns are rising out of his thick dreadlocks.

Sam steadies herself and then sets off slowly down the hill. I hesitate, then follow. When we get to camp Cap drops into a foldout chair its thin aluminum frame trembles under his weight. Sam seats herself on a log on the other side of the fire. I take a seat next to her.

"The fucking food has all gone to shit," Cap says, breaking the silence. He picks a mushy tomato from a bag at his feet and hurls it into the fire. "It's all rotten and mealy. I'm back to eating nothin' but these goddamn, fucking Go-Bars. Makes it feel like I'm passing a brick when I try to take a shit. Backs up my ass for days."

Sam and I stare into the fire, doing our best to avoid engaging with Cap. I feel the heat of his gaze on my face as he searches for a sparring partner. The fire pops sending sparks swirling between us.

Finally, Sam looks up, "Are there any left?"

Cap huffs and points towards the shack. Sam enters it then quickly returns with two and another jug of water. It's nacho cheese. I take a clumpy bite and think about how many of these things I have consumed in my life.

The answer is thousands.

The answer is depressing.

My best friend in middle school had a joke, "What do you call cheese that's not yours? Not-Yo-Cheese."

A disembodied smile creeps across my face, splitting my lips in a way I had forgotten was possible. "Not-Yo-Cheese." I pass my thumb over the familiar packaging. I don't mind Go-Bars, I guess. I don't mind any of this enough to do what is being planned on my behalf.

Sam rips off a hunk with her back teeth, chewing it like a dog with an oversized bone. "We went through the target today. It should be an easy rig and will come down, like really spectacularly. It'll make a huge dust cloud people will see for miles." She doesn't mention all the sleeping people inside.

Cap only snorts in response. Finished with his cigar, he throws the butt into the fire, pulls a toothpick out from behind his right ear, and leans back in the flimsy folding chair, twiddling the toothpick back and forth between his lips. He stops for a second to dig out a chunk of Go-Bar from his molars. It too is flung unceremoniously into the fire.

Sam waits for him to settle and continues, "Anyway, I think we need something mobile. There are cameras all over the building, and they've already had a good look at my face. So, if you could design something that can be launched or whatever, that would be best. I don't want to get too close again."

"Like a rocket?"

Sam perks up, "Yeah! Can you build that?"

"No, I can't build you a fucking rocket. What the fuck do you think I am?" Cap snaps, "Shit."

Sam shrinks, "Well maybe you could rig an old car or truck and we could stick the gas pedal and drive it through the front window."

Cap sucks on his teeth and stares into the flames. "You'll use whatever I tell you to use. I don't need any goddamn tips on how to blow up a fucking building." Cap shifts his weight and points his chin at me, "You really are dumb as dog shit, aren't you?"

I am going to run away - tomorrow. I am going to run away as fast as I can. I'll get up before Sam does her karate routine and just never come back. I'll find the river with my nose and follow it out until it leads me back to town. Then I'll go talk to the police or whoever cares about this bullshit, tell them everything and go back to my little apartment and enjoy my Go-Bars and Power Flakes by myself in the dark, and play my video games until I die. That'll be it. That's the plan.

Cap stares at me through the fire. His eyes burn hot like flaming pokers, gouging out my eyeballs with naked hatred.

"You don't see anything wrong with any of this do you?" he asks, waiting for a response. When I offer none, he continues, "Man, you *are* stupid. I don't have any sympathy for stupid."

"Cap! Keep it together. We're almost through," Sam shouts.

With a humph, Cap unfolds his massive frame off the chair and towers over me. He looks down chewing on his toothpick contemplatively.

"I'll have your shit tomorrow. I'm going to bed." Turning his back to me, Cap lumbers out of the range of the fire and disappears into the night.

Sam faces me and smiles. She reads my expression and the smile slides off her face. Reaching into her sweatshirt, she pulls out the notebook and flips quickly through it with her thumb and forefinger, looking for just the right quote to put my poor little heart at ease.

The thought of hearing another great revolutionary speak to me from beyond the grave, coaxing me towards greatness like a zombie football coach, fills me with pure dread. It makes my head swim.

I grab Sam's wrist, stopping the pages from fluttering. She looks up, surprised that I initiated contact. My cells steel themselves to resist her at a molecular level, straining hard against every instinct that has been ingrained in them.

"I'm going to bed," I say.

I let her wrist go, get up, and leave the fire. Cap is still nowhere to be seen. I settle myself onto the bare floor of the shack, the air inside is stale and feels hot against the coolness of the surrounding night. This will be my last night here, I promise myself that much.

CHAPTER THIRTEEN

Like Piss

The first tendrils of light crept their way through the forest, crawling around the sleeping trees, waking up the birds that remained through the encroaching coldness of fall. Too cowardly to lose myself in these woods in the dark, I wrestled through the sleepless night, waiting desperately for a sign of dawn.

The campsite is silent and slick with dew. I unfold myself from the old sleeping bag as quietly as possible and survey the landscape. There is no sign of Cap and no stirring of Sam from inside her tent. A light fog snakes its way along the debris of summer's leaves that coat the ground.

Time to make a break for it. I take a step out of the shack; my feet crunching on the twigs and leaves underfoot. Panic flows out of my heart, pulling the skin tightly across my face. Searching for some sign of movement, I stop and squint through the poor light at Sam's tent. She doesn't stir. I wait for a ten count, holding my breath, watching with bulging eyes. Nothing happens.

Choosing my steps carefully, I negotiate the path worn across camp, granting a wide birth to Sam's tent. The fire has burned down to ashes, the last of the smoke rises against the wet morning. Despite my best efforts, dead branches snap and pop as I cross the bottom of our ravine and scramble up the hill that rings our little hell. I check for movement over my shoulder but don't stop.

Reaching the top, I pause and look down. A sense of relief washes over my body, scrubbing my bones of their weary exhaustion. I turn and look elated at the dense woods in front of me. I feel like grabbing a tree around the trunk and skipping about in an ecstatic circle with one arm ringing the bark, the other pointed towards the sky in victory.

This is it.

The caged bird has finally flown the coop.

I take my first hesitant steps towards freedom, it feels good, so good that I take another and another. Soon the camp is a hundred yards behind me, then more. The morning light grows brighter bathing the woods, beautiful and alive. Flies unfold themselves from their hiding places and set about the hard work of buzzing around. Small birds, finches or chickadees, bounce from branch to branch, flying about in short spastic bursts of energy, happy to be alive on such a beautiful day.

Behind me something crashes through the underbrush, going from left to right. Shattered, I whirl around on my heel expecting the worst, expecting pink.

Instead, I see a white-tailed deer dart across my trail. It prances lightly, working its way around the trees and bushes with feet nimbler than mine.

The deer runs past and stops about ten yards in front of me, chewing on greenery. It is the most beautiful animal I have ever seen. I creep up behind it, watching its ears twitch as they track the sounds of my footsteps. I expect it to run but it doesn't. This is a sign. Things like this only happen to princesses in Disney movies.

The deer turns sideways and watches me with one large almond-shaped eye. Inching closer, within five feet now, I am going to try to touch it, maybe I'll be able to ride it. I take another step closer and grab a handful of leaves from the last of the green shrubbery, a peace offering - reaching out my hand, my fingers strain, pushing the snack towards the animal's soft back.

He tilts his head, two small horns rise just above his ears, and it takes a step back to turn and face me head-on. I stop my approach. The deer and I stand in front of each other, waiting for something.

Without warning, he spreads his back legs apart, dropping his hips towards the ground, and releases a thick stream of steaming yellow piss. This seems to be the only way the animal kingdom communicates with me. The deer stares at me brazenly, eye to eye. I take a step backward and the pee stops as abruptly as it started.

I take two more steps backward, and the deer lowers his head and trots forward, pawing and stamping the ground aggressively as he closes the gap between us. A loud snort escapes his nose as he drags a hoof across the dirt that separates us.

I am not Snow White.

Seeing that I have not removed myself from his presence with the appropriate amount of panic, the young buck lowers his stubby little antlers and charges headlong towards me. My reflexes are slow. The buck catches me cleanly along the right side, in my ribs. He whinnies in triumph as the air is driven out of me, sending me to the ground with a painful thud. My vision doubles and bursts into stars as I scramble to my feet and continue to retreat.

Annoyed by my pigheadedness, the animal charges at me again. This time I run, wildly sprinting away from him as fast as my wounded lungs allow. Emboldened by the chase and possibly the chance to turn the tables on the age-old relationship between predator and prey, the animal catches me after a dozen steps, hitting me firmly in my kidneys, sending pain spiraling through my nerves.

No longer satisfied with trying to gore me with its little antlers, the deer rears up on its hind legs and begins thrashing me with his front hooves. I cover my head tightly with my arms as the blows rain down and do the only thing left to do, scream. The sound I'm making is different than what I produced in the halls of Mike Michaels campaign headquarters - it is throaty, less shrill, more primal, like the scream a caveman would make while battling a saber tooth tiger to the death. This is progress. I am proud of myself.

The buck, undisturbed by my commotion but apparently frustrated by the limited damage being done to my head, aims lower and lands one cloven hoof deep into my solar plexus. The air whooshes out of my body like a strong gust of wind and my manly battle cry ceases. He pauses and celebrates by releasing another storm of piss onto my feet.

My tongue flops around in my mouth, desperate to pull some oxygen back into my withered lungs. I do the only thing I can and roll over onto my stomach, offering up my back but protecting my most sensitive, private bits while waiting for sweet death at the hands of the tender forest creature.

I wonder who will find my body and what they will suppose became of me. Who would suspect my skull was caved in by a timid young deer? Perhaps the police will find my half-frozen corpse, decaying under the first few inches of snow, and hire a wildlife biologist to speculate about what animal in these woods could have caused such damage. Maybe there will be murmurs of a Bigfoot and locals will have a fun time providing hopeful quotes to naive strangers.

If my death can be a boon to tourism, that would be more help to the world than I ever offered while still alive. I guess a tangible legacy is the best any of us can hope for.

While I wait patiently for one of the buck's striking hoofs to pop my head like an overripe melon, I hear a loud sound crashing towards us. It sounds like a bear, possibly looking to make two meals in one - venison stuffed with man meat or perhaps, Go-Bar marinated boy-kabobs skewered on deer antler with bone marrow dressing. Either way, we'll be delicious, I'm sure.

The headline crystallizes in my head - Local Man Provides Final Meal to Bear Before Long Hibernation. Most Useful He Ever Was.

So much for the mysterious death.

So much for my contribution to local lore and humanity.

The crashing closes in and the deer screams, making a sound like tires squealing along a blacktop. I squeeze my eyes tighter imagining the huge beast with its jaws wrapped around the deer's slender neck, its eyes bulging and tongue swaying as it struggles against death. I wait for the hot splatter of deer blood on my back and then for the searing pain from a sharp claw ripping into my flesh. The paw reaches down and grabs the back of my shirt, stretching the cotton across my neck as it pulls me upwards. Nature is so confusing.

"Get the fuck up, stupid," a voice hisses. Cap stands over me, straddling me between his legs.

The buck stands in front of him, rubbing at its face with a front hoof. It shakes its head and stares at us with a boiling hatred.

"Don't try me again," Cap warns.

The deer shakes the cobwebs, lowers its head, and stumbles towards us. I scramble underneath Cap's legs putting him between me and the stubby antlers. Cap grits his teeth, dips his hips, digging the soles of his combat boots into the soil, and meets the deer in the middle, shoulder directly underneath its chin. The animal makes the tire squealing noise again and hops about madly, its mouth coated in bloody spit.

"Fuckin' told you so," Cap says straightening up.

Frustrated, the deer pounds the ground again with his front hooves and sneers, blowing a bloody snot bubble. Cap spits on the ground between us and flexes his enormous fists.

"Go on, fucking git!"

The deer looks us over once more, then admits defeat and bounds off into the woods. Cap turns and looks me up and down, his nose crinkles, "You smell like piss."

He's right.

"Bucks will fuck you up if you make 'em mad enough, especially the young ones. They're all full of testosterone. You're lucky he didn't have his full rack. What the hell are you doing all the way out here?"

I open my mouth before my brain is ready to reply. It hangs open for a while and then closes with a snap when I come up empty. Cap watches me struggle against myself and his eyes soften.

"You trying to escape that pink-haired crazy down there?"

I look out into the forest longingly. The sun has risen above the horizon and the dew is beginning to evaporate. I didn't make it very far from the camp. I take a final deep breath of the fresh morning air and nod to Cap.

"You should have gone a long time ago. You should have left weeks ago, right when you got here, when there was a genuine chance she would have let you go. If you still want to go. I'll let you. I'll cover for you and pretend like this never happened." Cap pauses and breaths deeply of the cool morning air. He looks around the forest wistfully. "But know this, she'll find you. She's good at that, and I won't stop her. I won't be able to. You should have gotten out when I told you to go, while you had the chance."

"I . . . I can go to the cops," I stammer.

Cap shakes his head. "You can but it won't do any good, and she will still find you. She found others smarter, faster, and stronger than you. She buried them all." Cap gives me a hand to my feet and shrugs. "It is what she does."

"What should I do? Sam says she wants me to do something horrible. There are people in that Michaels' building. Rooms full of people. I can't go through with this."

Cap fumbles through his pockets and pulls out the day's first cigar. He leans against a tree, lights it, and looks me over.

"The way I see it, there are only two options for you. You either do what she says, or you die." He takes a deep pull from the cigar and blows the smoke slowly out of his nose. "What I suggest you do is make her think you are dead."

"How do I do that?"

"It won't be easy," Cap says exhaling another cloud. "But I know a way." He frowns and stamps out the lit end of the cigar on the tree, being careful not to ruin the unsmoked portion. "It's cold and I'm not gonna stand around here all-day jabbering. So, you coming back or taking your chances out here on your own?"

My knees wobble and my breath shortens. Cap raises his eyebrows and makes the choice for me. "Come on, follow me."

He turns and lumbers off the way he came. I wait a second and then follow in his giant footsteps.

CHAPTER FOURTEEN

Doom

When we get back to the camp, Cap gets to work. He tells Sam that he underestimated how long he would need. It takes him the better part of three days to fully construct the explosive we're, I'm, supposed to use to blow up Michaels' headquarters.

Sam and I hardly see him and when we do, he stomps around us, angry and yelling about the quality of the food and what a piece-of-shit I am. He rolls out of camp as quickly as he rolls in. I never see where he goes. He doesn't mention our conversation in the woods, doesn't give me an acknowledgment that there is another plan or that he is trying to help. Maybe he was setting me up by getting me to come back here. I don't have enough courage stored up to confront him or to attempt a second escape.

During the nights I have a recurring dream. There is a room. It is full of beds covered in white sheets with small lumps rising and falling on top. Flames start on the floor and spread up the walls quickly catching the sheets.

As the heat intensifies, starting in the back of the room, each of the lumps on the beds pops like a balloon. The fire surges towards me, pop, pop, pop. I look down and I'm holding a can of lighter fluid with both my hands. I spray it all over the floor in a path back to my feet. The flames follow the track to my feet quickly enveloping me. The fire burns pink as the flesh melt off my bones.

*   *   *

Sam and I pass the days together tending to the camp during the day and the fire at night. She tries to start conversations, but no matter the topic, I can never think of anything to say. She doesn't ask me what I was doing when the deer attacked me.

I don't know what Cap told her, maybe everything. I don't particularly care. I adjust. This becomes my new normal. I wake up, watch Sam exercise, get the morning drinking water, collect firewood, eat a Go-Bar, avoid Cap, and slowly burn the sticks until it becomes dark enough to sleep again. I exist like a slug underneath a log. Not asking questions has become my superpower.

One day, I wake up to a drizzle. It patters on the roof of the shack, rousing me from my light sleep before the sun comes up. Flipping over on my stomach, I survey the soggy campsite.

Sam's tent unzips and she sticks her head out and looks at the sky, her hair glowing like magic in the struggling light. She sees me staring and leans forward, hands on her chin, returning my gaze. My eyes swim in and out of focus as she smiles at me. It makes me want to throw up.

Despite everything my mind can't help but wander back to my apartment, watching her in the shower. It's too much and I have to roll over on my back, eyes on the ceiling. I consider the noble slug – hermaphrodite, slimy, unconcerned, role model.

I stay on my back staring up at the ceiling as the rain drones across the roof. Eventually, I drift back into my troubled sleep filled with the dreams of fires and the people that I used to know.

"Wake-the-fuck-up."

My eyes flutter open, confused. Cap towers over me, chewing on his toothpick. He nudges me with one huge combat boot, a little too forcefully. I scramble up into a seated position and try to quickly wipe the sleep from my brain. It's pitch black and the fire has burned down. Slowly burning embers provide the only light. Sam is nowhere to be seen. Cap sits on his haunches bringing his face within inches of mine.

"I went into town last night and looked at the building." His breath is hot on my face. "The brick is old as shit and will crumble easily. Piece of cake."

"Did you tell Sam?" I gulp.

"Tell her what? About you trying to run away? Fuck no," Cap says.

"Listen, tomorrow I'm going to give you a backpack and a switch. The switch will have two settings. You hit it once and the bag will make a big pop and some fire will fizz out of it. You keep that shit on your back, hit the switch, fall, and stay down. No theatrics. Seeing that, she's not going to come look you over I can guarantee you that." Cap leans back and scratches his chin.

"What happens if I hit the switch twice?"

Cap smiles widely. In the dark, I hear it more than I see it. "If you hit it twice, then the thing works as intended and the building comes down. You decide to hit it twice, best to make sure it's not on your back first." His knees pop as he stands up. "Sam's been right all along about one thing; it's up to you to make the decision."

He lumbers off into the night and there is nothing but the stillness of the forest. Lying on my back I stare up at the unseen, rotting ceiling.

This time sleep doesn't come. At least not in a way I have ever slept before. It's something else that overtakes me. Time passes, I think, but there is no way to discern it. My mind wanders, racing frantically, overwhelming itself. Raindrops fall like a metronome on the roof of my shack.

I feel sick, feverish, but my forehead is cool to the touch. Eventually, the sky lightens, slowly at first, and then the day picks up speed. My brain calms, mercifully slowing and my eyes finally close exhausted. Colors explode like fireworks against the backdrop of my closed eyelids, worming back and forth across my vision. I watch them swim across my eyes like beautiful snakes slithering inside my skull. They are better than any other thought I've had in weeks.

The color snakes are shattered when a hand materializes out of the darkness and shakes my shoulder.

"Hurry up. Time to get this shit over with."

Cap turns and leads back towards the fire. The rain has stopped, but clouds are stitched across the sky, blocking any hint of the sun, making it impossible to estimate what time it is. Sam sits on a wet log, poking at some dead coals with a long stick.

"Hey there sleepy head!" she says brightly, her eyebrows arching.

I try to let the words wash over me but to no effect. In an act of unforgivable betrayal, my heart overloads my capillaries sending blood rushing to my cheeks in a bright blush. Sam notices and smiles triumphantly. It's not for the reason she thinks, and I turn my head away from her, stretching out on the other side of the fire, avoiding eye contact.

Cap saunters in front of us and gently places a new black backpack on the ground before taking a seat. "There it is," he says gruffly, "Don't fucking drop it or shake it too much."

Sam gingerly picks up the pack turning it over in her hands, admiring Cap's handiwork. She reaches for the zipper.

"The fuck did I just say? Leave it alone," Cap reprimands sitting bolt upright in his chair. Sam's hand pauses on the zipper and then let's go.

Cap snarls, "Be careful with that shit. Drop it in front of the building and get the fuck out of the way before you press the little button or stand right next to it and barbecue your ass, I don't give a shit, but be fucking careful of that fucking thing around me, understood?"

Cap reaches into his pocket and fishes out a small, black, rectangular plastic cube. One grey thumb-sized button is embedded in the middle. He hands it to Sam, who tucks it into her sweatshirt. Cap looks at me quickly and then back into the fire.

Sam places the pack on the ground and frowns, "You're not going to come with us?"

"The fuck you need me for?" Cap bristles. "You and your boyfriend over there have got this one locked up. Just put that bad boy in position and get the fuck out of the way. It'll work fine, trust me. Get way the fuck away from it or your asses will be turned into meat sauce." Cap nods at me. "That thing goes off around you and they'll bring you home in a jar."

I watch Sam out of the corner of my eye. She pauses, soaking Cap in, considering how to respond. Creases deepen on her forehead as her eyebrows converge towards the bridge of her nose.

Cap watches her trying to process all this. He pulls a cigar from a pocket in his pants, lights it, and blows the sweet-smelling smoke at us.

The computer in Sam's head sorts through the situation and recalibrates. The tension across her forehead eases and the slight smile returns to her lips. I wish the computer in my head worked the same way, sorting and resorting and planning. Somewhere along the way, my motherboard was fried and now all it does is fret and worry and accept.

Sam carefully picks up the pack, wrapping her arms through both straps. It's heavy and pulls tightly at her neck. She looks like a homicidal turtle.

"You ready?" she asks me cheerily.

My skull recoils at the suggestion that I may be ready for whatever it is I am supposed to be an accomplice to. I look around wildly, searching for some reason to delay or distract. There are only trees and pine needles around me, all excuses are inconveniently absent. Sam shifts the pack around her neck and waits for me to respond.

She notices I lack sufficient motivation and rustles through her baggy sweatshirt until she fishes out her ragged notebook. I want to rip it from her little hands and throw it in the fire or eat it or anything but listen to another nauseating passage from someone long-dead but still more present than me. Maybe I should jump on her, forcing her backward onto that pack - ending this.

She flips through the pages, stopping finally with her thumb.

"Sometimes you have to pick the gun up to put the gun down. - Malcolm X."

Cap snorts loudly, rattling all the loose phlegm in his nasal passage, drawing it into his mouth before firing off a large yellow loogie into the fire.

"Now you're both just wasting time. Get a move on it," he commands.

Sam shifts the weight of the pack and starts up the hill. Left with a choice between Cap and the pink-haired maniac likely on her way to commit murder, I choose murder and follow her up the hill.

Quickly we're immersed deep in the woods again and I'm familiarly lost. We walk through the cloudy morning in silence. Each step I take rustles the leaf-strewn ground in the same way.

Cap's instructions play over and over in my mind. I imagine that the sound of my feet against decaying matter is really the universe asking me, "what are you doing?" over and over again. The cosmic message quickly wipes out all other thoughts.

whatareyoudoing?

whatareyoudoing?

whatareyoudoing?

I change up my footsteps, trying to break the spell and add a bit of a shuffle with my toes to each step. The message shifts to:

whyareyoudoingthis

whyareyoudoingthis

whyareyoudoingthis

This isn't working. I concentrate on shortening my footfall to a straight up and down motion. The universe responds with:

youarefucked

youarefucked

youarefucked

Madness is scratching at the inside of my frontal lobe, clawing its way inside my big broken computer. This all seems ridiculous and poorly planned. People are going to get hurt. We're going to get caught.

I assemble whatever courage remains cowering inside me and catch up with Sam, pulling even with her. "This seems like a bad idea. It's broad daylight. There are people and cameras everywhere. Also, I'm not sure there is ever a time when people aren't inside the building."

I feel that these points are all reasonable.

Sam's eyebrows raise as her face contorts into a smirk, surprised in the way a parent is surprised when their child comes home from school with the multiplication tables memorized.

"Don't worry," she soothes. "This pack probably isn't big enough to take down the back half of the building. We'll just crumble the front facade and blast that fucking hologram into space." She reads the skepticism on my face and adds, "We'll figure out a way to detonate it on the sidewalk in front, so the entire building doesn't come down. I've done this before." She grins, lying.

Such is my contribution to humanity, to the cause of our freedom and enlightenment, to the shedding of our bondage - the destruction of a live-action cartoon and public nuisance will be conducted with the utmost responsibility and care.

Sam squirms again under the weight of the bomb strapped to her back, "Would you mind carrying this for a while? It's starting to dig into my shoulders."

I look at the pack skeptically. *What's the difference?* Sam smiles appreciably at my openness and passes the backpack to me. Wincing, I slide it over my shoulders.

"Thanks," Sam says rolling her shoulders in relief.

The sun seems to choose this exact moment to break through the clouds. Light rings her pink head. She nestles up against my arm and smiles, batting her eyes. I accept the obvious manipulation without protest. The universe has very clearly chosen sides against me. She takes my hand, lacing our fingers together and we walk through the forest like lovers.

Her touch is cold, like death. Connected to her, my arm feels heavy like it's ready to fall off. Every part of my body is being stretched to its limits. She smiles in my face and squeezes my hand reassuringly.

"Everything is going to be great," she coos, patting the back of my hand. "You're going to do great."

I do my best to focus on Cap's instructions, picturing my carcass lying on the ground with fireworks exploding out of the backpack, playing dead. If I wasn't confronted with it as my best option, I would laugh at its ridiculousness.

Doom stretches out in front of me, through the sleeping trees, around the banks of a dead river, into a town full of tired rage and sullen exhaustion, wrapped snugly into a dirty sweatshirt, pulling me by the hand with a grin. I let it happen because that's what I'm supposed to do. Like my father said of me, I am a "good boy."

This is the story of the end of my life.

CHAPTER FIFTEEN

Pink Turtles

Together, hand-in-hand, Sam and I stomp through the forest. She is alive, sing-songing a plan to me that changes from step to step, re-analyzed and revised in real-time based on whatever whim makes its way across her cluttered pink brain.

At first, I listen intently, hoping to carve out some important detail that could save me, but it quickly becomes apparent that it is all bullshit. It's funny because I personally witnessed her execute two of these missions flawlessly. It's not funny because it is readily apparent that she has no plan.

Listening to her patter becomes exhausting. I would rather decide what to do at the last second and enjoy my remaining few moments of freedom now than burn up any more of my sanity examining all the reasons why this is a bad idea.

She has worn me out. I'm threadbare - full of holes. Sam uses the word "ballistic" then arcs her hand not intertwined in mine, through the air to illustrate a point about "trajectory."

These are important lessons. She really wishes Cap had built us a rocket.

A cool breeze flows in, rustling the bare branches in the thicket, swirling around us, enveloping me in fall and tickling my nostrils. A pair of mourning doves roosting in the brush take flight when we get too close to their home, lifting off noisily, winging up to the top of a birch tree.

I run my spare hand along the trunk of their tree as we pass, feeling the rough paper-ness of its bark. I clutch a piece, peel it off and turn it over and over in my hand before crushing it into a fine dust between my fingers.

Everything out here serves as a cruel reminder that amidst all the bleakness the world is still capable of beautiful moments. There is an air of finality hanging over our walk to town. I feel like a scientist, meticulously documenting every sensation no matter how mundane. This is why human animals never developed foresight, we're too dramatic.

Sam says the word "shockwave" or maybe it's two words, "shock wave." Her off-hand again spins around her head, illustrating some point about "safety radius." She grips my palm tighter and stares wildly into my eyes, sweaty with excitement. Insanity swims behind her pupils. She says the word "important" punctuating whatever point she is making with the word "proud."

Tears well up in my eyes. Sam thinks it's in response to her encouragement, so she spins me around and hugs me tightly. My arms stay pinned to my sides so I can't hug her back. Her lips brush against my ear as she whispers something unintelligible.

The dam breaks free and large wet tears cascade down my face. Sam squeezes me tighter, her eyes rolling back into her skull in ecstasy. Driven into a frenzy she must be imagining herself standing before the wretched masses of humanity, inspiring them to kill or revolt or think or give of themselves, just like all the famous people in her little black notebook, and I can't do anything but standby blankly in front of her crying.

I think I'm crying for selfish reasons, knowing I am doomed, either to splinter my meat and bones into a thousand little pieces or to splinter someone else's meat and bones into a thousand little pieces. But maybe the origin of the tears really is an inspiration, like Sam hopes.

Maybe I *am* a warrior for the future, destined for the scrolls of history, remembered as a liberator and mind-expander. Maybe, unbeknownst to me, the past week living in the company of Sam and Cap in the woods has been a training ground, cultivating a steel inside me I won't feel until pressed into action. Maybe Cap's foolish plan will work. Maybe if I turn myself into a human-sparkler, Sam will leave me alone.

"This is going to be amazing," she says assuredly.

My stomach drops into my knees and I can't look Sam in the eyes. The answer turns out to be self-pity. I am crying in self-pity, mourning the impending loss of me.

She raises a hand to my cheeks and delicately wipes a tear off my face. Her jaw quivers while her eyes, bulging with earnestness, search my face, misinterpreting my fear for righteous fire.

Cupping my face between both of her hands, Sam forces me to look her in the eyes, "You're going to be great. You are ready," she lies. This is a great moment for her.

We resume traipsing through the forest, following the banks of the dead river back to town. She spends the last hours of my life, puking up detail after detail, filling out a skeletal plan for how I'm supposed to blow up a building with a backpack while escaping with both my life and my freedom.

She lays out the path for me, jumping between alleys and buildings, before laying the pack at the foot of the entrance, supposedly the campaign center's "soft spot." Then she details my path out including the exact moment I depress the button and trigger the explosives. She must have a photographic memory. I continue ignoring her as much as I can.

I come up with my own plan. I'm going to cover my face and throw the backpack at the door from as far away as I can and then run quickly in the opposite direction.

My plan took only seconds to devise, and I'm sure it is just as good as the homicidal rantings Sam has spewed over the past few hours, or the supposed exit-plan that Cap devised for me.

We approach the scar in the earth created by Sam and Cap when they first blew up the rusted, old metal bridge. Ahead of us is the dead neighborhood, houses long abandoned to escape the smell of the then just-polluted river. The charred, black husks of three of the homes sit on their tired foundations, still smoldering from god-knows when. Sam guides us past the bridge, gurgling in its sludge-y, green coffin, and heads past the smoking houses without a word or acknowledgment of her handiwork.

She picks the old white clapboard house where I watched and filmed her the first time. I can't tell if she does it deliberately, a reunion of sorts. Her face doesn't betray her intentions. I'm not sure how she would know in any case. I follow her up on the old porch, picking past the rotten floorboards.

The white paint on one side is bubbled and scorched from the heat of the neighboring fires. Sam takes a seat facing the river with her back up against the side of the house. I take a seat next to her.

"We should hang out here until it gets darker," she explains.

A breeze drifts up from the clogged river, carrying the now-familiar scent of death with it. Like every other time, it slams my nose with the force of a baseball bat. I squeeze my eyes tight and sneeze.

"It's a lot to get used to," Sam says waving her hands at the house husks and the green river beyond.

Her eyes are watery as she holds the back of her hand over her nostrils. The stench lingers for a second before a breeze whips it around the house again and back through the rest of the abandoned neighborhood, rattling the old window frames in the houses like a rambunctious pair of ghosts.

I shiver and settle back in against the old siding. This place gives me the creeps. I run my fingers across the old wood of the floorboards, picking at some splintered pieces of wood. I try to commit this feeling to memory, cataloging it alongside the other mundanities I have spent half a life taking for granted. These hours before darkness descends on us are like a last meal for the senses.

"Want to hear a story?" Sam asks.

I don't.

"Are you curious about where I came from?"

Some people communicate only in rhetorical questions - in any case, I'm not curious.

Sam licks her lips, eyes glittering in excitement or blood lust or both, and begins, "I grew up in California, back before the Colorado River completely dried up. We had a big house, one of those classic California, post-modern style ranches. We had a large yard and a dog, a handsome golden retriever."

I keep my eyes focused on the floor. This is not how I want to spend the remaining few precious moments of my life. Maybe Sam will figure out how to read body language.

Instead, she continues, "When I was young it was great. There wasn't enough water for us to grow grass, but my mom did some beautiful things with rocks and cacti. The government restricted how much water every household could use. All the greywater in our house, you know, like the stuff that came out of a faucet, would run through these filters, and be recycled to fill up the toilets or whatever. I just remember it was hot, really hot, but it just felt, you know, normal or whatever. I was a kid. I didn't know any different or any better."

The breeze from the river returns, blasting us with a fresh punch of putridity. Sam's nostrils flex, but she works through it, continuing her little life story, misunderstanding my focused silence as interest.

"It was a great life," she sighs wistfully, eyes off in the distance, remembering whatever she was before she became this. "It was my brother. He was the first one in my neighborhood, but it happened to lots of others too. The wastewater would flow through the filters and collect in this big tub that took up almost half of our basement. The old water would mix with the new water and that's how we lived. But the government just kept reducing the amount of new water each family was allocated every month."

Sam pauses, a dark slug of snot descending down on to her upper lip. She sniffs, sending the slime shooting back up into her nose. It's unclear if the leak is from the toxic stench or the unnecessary trip down her memory lane.

"Anyway, at some point, there was no new water coming in and with the whole system tied together the filters could only do so much."

I remember what this was now. I remember when this happened. For a moment my concentration breaks and I let Sam's words in. She sniffs up another nasal leak.

"I mean we had rations of bottled water to drink and my mom would boil the water that came out of the faucets before she used it in food, but I guess there was just too much to keep track of, too many variables to account for. So first it was my brother, maybe he kept his mouth open in the shower or maybe it just made its way through his pores, or something, I don't know ..." Sam's voice drifts off.

This was a big deal on the news. As the droughts strangled California, thousands of people, maybe more, became ill marinating in their own filth. My third-grade class organized a bottle drive, where we collected and donated a few hundred cases of clean bottled water and shipped it off to their state.

"It was awful to watch him just sort of wither away. He was in the hospital for weeks before my parents took him home. They gave him some medicine and fluids and stuff, but nothing could get him over the hump. The worst part was looking into his eyes and knowing he understood what was happening to him and seeing him accepting it." Sam sniffs again.

She pauses and I look up quickly from making toothpicks out of the soft floorboards.

Sam's face is pinched, her brow furrowed tightly as she bites dramatically on her bottom lip. I watch cautiously out of the corner of my eye, drawn in but not wanting to give any encouragement to continue the show. Sam chews some more on her lip then sighs. The cloud across her face passes as the tension in her forehead eases. She smiles and refills the machine inside her with quarters, ratcheting up the chipper dial.

"So that's pretty much what set me on the path I'm on now."

A dead kid brother back-story seems a tad melodramatic, but I guess it's as good an excuse as any for our upcoming mass murder. I'm just glad the truth portion of our little game is over. I already know what the dare entails.

We sit together on the porch, stewing in our silence, together but alone. Eventually, Sam turns to her journal, flipping through page after page, breaking the quiet with some of her muted mumblings.

I decide to use the time wisely, scheming obsessively about how to get out of this putrid task. From experience, I know my internal fight or flight mechanism is thoroughly broken. My body's only exports, it seems, are crippling indecision and flatulence - my gross national product. An entire life's work, so far, has consisted entirely of humiliation and nervous farting. I quickly rip through the most obvious options:

Throwing the whole mess, backpack, and detonator, into the green river?

Sam still has the detonator. Somehow, I'd have to get the pack and detonator away from her while we're down here. And there's still no exit plan beyond that.

Or I could find the nearest cop, throw myself at their feet, and beg for safety?

Counterproductive. Sam seems to exist outside of consequences, and I'm sure by this point, I've probably broken some important law. Also, despite going back and forth a half dozen times, I couldn't lead anybody to the campsite.

My brain is not impressive. This whole experience with Sam and Cap has reinforced this singularly important lesson - I've been stuck with a poor version of the calculator everyone else is carrying around on top of their meat. It seems broken and strange in every important possible way it could be broken or strange.

Any delusions I've ever had of achieving even an averageness have been shattered. Focusing all my computing power on what should be a simple problem has yielded only one acceptable result, to listen to Cap's plan, hope the sight of me on fire is enough to dissuade Sam from ever thinking of me again, and when the coast is clear, run as fast as I can in whatever is the opposite direction of where she is.

I'm going to run until my lungs explode, avoiding the woods or any sort of wooded area at all costs. I'll stay under the streetlights and when I can't run anymore, I'll lie down in the middle of the street and wait for daylight to break. Then I'll force my pitiful little brain to think up an entirely new plan for what to do next.

This plan is feeble, but it is the best I can do. One shouldn't expect water to come from stones just like one shouldn't expect a genius to come from the mishmash of underdeveloped grey flesh, and whatnot, that's sloshing around in my skull.

My heart picks up the pace, beating erratically against its rib cage. I can hear blood pumping like a raging river through my veins. Adrenaline reaches every corner of my body, putting me at an uncomfortable level of alert. I look down at the back of my hand, it's shaking like an alcoholic. The anticipation is the worst part. Sam is still fully immersed in the musings contained in her journal and doesn't seem to notice my rapidly deteriorating state.

The sun sets slowly behind us and darkness falls over the old house in a cold, wet blanket. When the last of the light extinguishes, Sam closes her notebook and retracts her limbs into her oversized sweatshirt - a psychotic, pink turtle, and without another word, she falls asleep.

There is a small amount of blood staining the old grey floorboards where we sit, where my mindless clawing has torn up the tips on my fingers. Sam snores lightly next to me and

I put the fingers into my mouth and suck on the blood. The sensation is comforting and before I have a chance to unpack why I lean over and nestle my head comfortably on Sam's sideways lap. Her hand meanders out from its cotton cocoon and finds its way onto my head, stroking my hair until I too drift off into a fitful sleep.

CHAPTER SIXTEEN

The Resistance

"Wake up."

I had a terrible dream.

"Wake up."

A small hand reaches through the ether of sleep and gently shakes my shoulder. What an awful dream. The cobwebs dissipate as relief washes over me. A sing-song voice coos sweetly into my ear, "Time to get up sleepy head."

I crack my eyes open, slightly. I am in my bed with the curtains drawn tightly blocking out all light from the street below. The scent of musty laundry strewn across my floor stings my nostrils. I should get up and get something to eat. It must be time for work.

"Come on - important work awaits," a small female voice pleads.

My eyes snap open and adjust, filling me back full of weary dread. What a terrible life. I pull my face off Sam's stomach and sit against the wall of the dilapidated squat house. She rustles my hair playfully and stands up, stretching, and yawning. The world around us outside the crumbling porch is dark and still.

"Come on," Sam says. "We're a short walk away. It's perfect."

My molars grind stressfully against each other as I stand up, rehashing the plan again in my mind. Sam hoists the pack onto her back, then looks up at me and smiles. "I'll carry it for the first leg so we can keep you limber."

She leads us off the porch, across the overgrown front lawn, and onto the silent street. Even in the pitch blackness, I make out the familiar graffiti covering the front door; ABANDON HOPE - a fitting post-script to my wasted life.

I follow Sam lifelessly along Main Street. We round a small hill, and I see the blocky facade of Michaels' Campaign headquarters in the distance.

We pass my old office building, sitting there silently in the dark, stewing with impotent rage.

We pass the twisted remains of the ration station, still sitting in its original spot, a reminder of something from before.

We pass the park benches where my pants were down. They are empty now, yet still pulse with menace and hatred.

My life doesn't need to flash before my eyes. Instead, these two blocks drag their ghosts out in front of me, a slow stream of reminders of a life wasted - a drip, drip, drip of regret.

Sam stops a hundred yards from the building, de-shoulders the pack, and passes it over to me. She fishes through her clothing and produces the small black switch, handing it to me gingerly. I accept it and run my thumb over the cool plastic button. Sam points towards the building and I nod. Yes, this is my mission. I have chosen to accept it.

She reaches up, grabs my collar, and pulls my face down to her level. She looks into my eyes then kisses me, one hand tugging on my collar, the other on the back of my head, pulling me deeply into her.

Unsurprised, I let all of this happen without resistance. I let her tongue explore my mouth. I reciprocate, darting lightly in and out of her. The kiss contains the framework for everything I have ever wanted in life, but it is empty, like a death row meal.

Sam lets go of me and steps back, then turns and disappears down an alley between two apartment buildings. She never bothered to tell me where I should meet back up with her after I presumably carry out her bidding. Details, I guess.

I turn away, back toward the headquarters. There is no sign of movement inside any of the windows. The street that runs by the front is abandoned. Beaming out from somewhere in the dark behind me, I feel Sam's eyes on my back, pushing me towards my destiny. I let my legs do their horrible work and close the remaining hundred yards quickly.

As I meet the building the hologram springs to life, shouting at me with its crazy eyes, shattering the silence of the street. My nerves are tattered. I wait in front of the building, holding the backpack in one sweaty hand, letting the psychotic, electric ghost rant above me. Air flows in and out of my lungs in raspy, ragged chunks.

Blocking out the noise, I wait to see if the hologram attracts any attention. The street remains still. No shades open. No new lights flicker on in any of the windows. The Michaels mirage resets itself, starting its blathering script from the top. I stop in front of him and look backward for Sam. There is no sign of her. The hair on my neck stands at attention. The building pulses in front of me, full of life. Behind the layers of glass and brick and steel, I feel a generation of misguided youth asleep between shifts, unaware of the plans for their martyrdom.

The detonator sits in my front pocket, heavy like a brick. Though I can't see her, I feel Sam watching me from her dark alleyway. There is no delaying it. Time for the show. I take a deep breath and push the button once. Something deep inside the bag whirs, clicks then falls silent. Nothing.

My skin crawls, screaming at me to drop the pack and run. Instead, I stand before the shrieking electric ghost and watch as my reflection in the mirror turns pale. Maybe I should hit the button again.

The bag shakes suddenly on my back, rattling my head back and forth on my thin neck, and then I am airborne, twirling through space. The sidewalk rises and I fall hard, banging my chin off the ground, grinding my teeth painfully.

The thing hisses menacingly and then erupts in flames, as it deposits me roughly onto the sidewalk. I scream with all the oxygen in my lungs as the fire heats up, igniting the shirt on my back, licking at my hair. The straps have my arms pinned. I wriggle and roll against it trying to work myself free, but there is no way to break the grip.

It hurts.

This is the price I am supposed to pay. Either I pay it with my life and finish up, or I trust Cap and play dead, hoping this façade is a façade. Even if it melts the skin off my back, that is the price of freedom.

Accepting this fate, I bite my lip and lie as still as death, unclear if I am waiting for the real thing to happen or just another actor in someone else's horrid play. The pack pops and hisses like the campfire, searching for dry fuel, some tinder to consume. It stops hurting and I wait for this experiment to wind down, ready for whatever comes next.

Footfalls ring against the glass front of the building. I think it's Sam coming to save me. I press my forehead into the pavement and pray for the fire to hurry up and find the traction it needs. For the first time, I notice the controller is still tucked safely in my hand. If we weren't so close to the headquarters, I would hit the button a second time as soon as she touches me, sending us both into the stratosphere.

"We got him!"

It isn't Sam's voice.

"Get him up."

A hand reaches down grabbing my shoulder, pulling me roughly back to my feet. Two men with black ski masks obscuring their faces turn me around to face them. My brain swims in my skull, threatening to turn out the lights. Visions of the two men float in front of me as I concentrate on staying awake.

One speaks into a small mic attached to the top of his shirt. "Yup, we have the package."

I wonder what the package is, me, or the backpack. I wish I had one of those masks. One of them peels the flaming pack gingerly off my back and holds it out away from his face.

He slaps violently at my back, brushing a gloved hand along my shirt and neck.

"Fire's out," he reports to someone, as he tucks the bag against the front wall of the headquarters.

The other one sticks his hands brusquely into the front pockets of my pants. He comes up empty and tries the backside. Nothing.

Frustrated, he whistles through his teeth, "Come on," and frisks me violently.

Not finding whatever he's looking for, he stands back and looks at his partner. They drag me around a corner away from the commotion of the sizzling bag and the Mike Michaels projection.

The partner steps forward and asks, " Where is the detonator?"

Sharp blond whiskers protrude from the mouth hole of both their face masks. Overworked, my brain scrambles to piece together what is happening.

Black spots dance across my eyes, clouding my vision. One of the radios strapped across their collar crackles again. I don't understand the garbled speak that comes out of the little black box.

One of them depresses a little button on the side and responds, "Working on it."

These are the twin cops who escorted me back to my apartment. I've been caught.

"I didn't set it off," I explain. My knees wobble and buckle. One of the men catches me before I can hit the ground again. "Thanks," I reply dumbly.

Patiently, the cop repeats, "Where is the detonator?"

I shouldn't admit to anything. The cops look me over, eyes bugging out of the holes in their masks. Both of their gazes settle on my fist, clenched tightly. I put my arm behind my back and hope that's enough for them to forget about it.

The cop grabs my wrist, yanking my arm upwards. His partner circles quickly behind me wrapping an arm around my neck, applying pressure to my jugular.

"Don't resist," he hisses, breath hot, like the fire on my neck.

The one in front of me pries my fingers open and examines the little rectangle sitting on my palm. "It's here," he transmits triumphantly into his little black box.

I am a dead man.

The arm on my neck tightens, constricting my windpipe. "Don't resist."

I didn't think I was. I wouldn't know how to, even if I were so inclined. If she was watching this scene, I wonder what quote Sam would be inspired to read from her little notebook.

His partner grasps my wrist tightly with one hand.

"I wasn't ever going to do it," I protest, rasping while the vice-like arm encircles my throat.

"Don't talk," commands the voice behind me.

The cop holding my wrist grabs my thumb with his other hand and folds it delicately over the edge of the button. He looks up from his work and nods to his partner. All the oxygen is quickly shut off to my brain, and as the lights flicker and dim, I can feel my thumb press down on the button.

A boom shatters the silence of the night, vibrating the pavement. I can't hold on to consciousness anymore and my body falls lightly to the ground.

Boom.

CHAPTER SEVENTEEN

Me, The Monster

The batter steps up to the plate. He grips the bat menacingly, squeezing it so hard I can see splinters break off and fall to the dirt under his cleats. The cotton sleeves of his pinstriped uniform flex and strain under stress from his rippling biceps.

I spit on the ground unimpressed and watch for the sign. Fastball. Of course. No one hits my fastball. Hiding the ball deep in my glove I take a four-seam grip and check the runner at third. He's not going anywhere.

I bare back down on the plate, concentrating on the center of the catcher's mitt, ready to unleash hell. My left leg rises, coiling my core into a tight spring. I unload the tension and fire a laser, painting the outside corner of the plate in blackness and despair.

"Steee-rike one!" the umpire yells, pointing to his left with one finger.

The capacity crowd cheers lustily as the numbers 1-0-1 flash up on the radar display hung above the scoreboard in right field.

Un-hittable.

The catcher shakes feeling back into his hand and softly tosses the ball to me. The batter taps the dirt out of his cleats with the barrel of the bat and digs into the box. He sneers towards the mound, baring gleaming white canine teeth. It's an empty gesture, borne of frustration and false confidence and I see right through it.

"Wake up."

The sign comes in. Curveball. Good, I have the best one in the business.

I check the runner on third. He hugs the bag, knees quaking in fear for what is about to come for his teammate at the plate. I don't blame him.

My fingers dig into the seams on the ball, and my body repeats the motion I've practiced thousands of times before, delivering my arm towards the plate with horrifying momentum.

At the last possible moment before releasing the ball, I rotate my wrist sharply, spinning the ball off my index finger. It arcs beautifully through the air cutting across the plate right to left like a bomb hurtling towards the earth.

This time the batter swings. But it's hopeless. His back leg gives out as he corkscrews himself into the ground.

"Steeeeee-rike two!" the umpire yells, rubbing salt into his wound.

The batter picks himself off the ground and dusts off his pants. He makes a good show of it, but I can tell by the gingerly way that he reaches down he pulled a muscle in his back flailing for that one.

"Son, wake up."

The catcher delivers the ball back to me. One more pitch. My arm feels alive. It tingles with anticipation. I'm waving off anything except fastball.

A park employee sitting behind the plate readies the radar gun, excited to be a small part of history.

Stepping off the rubber, I grab the resin bag and bounce it gently cross my right hand, milking the moment. I see my dad sitting behind the dugout, wearing my jersey. He smiles and raises one finger in the air - fastball.

"Jonesy, get the salts, will ya? This one's having a hard time coming out of it."

Stepping back up the mound, I grind my cleat into the dirt in front of the rubber and peer into the...

A sledgehammer slams up my nose and assaults the front of my brain, beating the lethargic grey sludge without mercy. My nose crinkles violently, forcing the skin on my forehead to peel back my eyelids. Cold, bright light flows in through my reluctant eyes, burning them worse than the punch up the nose.

"There he goes." A man sits in front of me.

When he sees my eyes open, he sits back and passes something in his hand to someone standing by the door behind him. There is a metal table between us. A harsh fluorescent light hangs above our heads, reflecting brightly off the table. The man nods his head, and his partner takes the package, places a box on the table then disappears out of the room.

"The twins brought you in. We've been watching you for a while. Doesn't look like they did too much damage subduing you. They said you were a wild one, but I guess that goes with the territory, eh?" He points towards my neck and winks.

I don't know what he is talking about. My neck is tender and it's difficult to swallow. He reaches into the box and pushes a bottle of water towards me. He watches in amusement as I take a sip and wince at the pain.

"A real wild one," he repeats. "Name's Buck. We met before in your apartment. After you took the video, right before you disappeared."

His hair is dark red, a thick orange mustache sits over his top lip. His skin is stark white and dotted with sun freckles.

"What happened?" I whisper.

My brain is still heavy with sleep. It feels like I've been drugged. I pick up the water for another sip but think better of it and screw the cap back on.

"What happened?" Buck snorts. "You went on a rampage. Took two of my best men to contain you. That's what happened. You're in a deep load of shit, son. Up to your eyeballs."

Rouge streaks start at Buck's ears and then break out across his face. His skin is a flashing billboard of emotion, betraying his mouth, unable to control the narrative put forth by his brain.

"Here," he says, reaching into the box and sliding a fresh pair of glasses across the table to me. I eye them suspiciously. "Go on," he prods, "put them on."

They look like a newer model than the pair I had that Cap crushed.

"Put 'em on."

I unfold them and slide them over my eyes. They vibrate pleasantly, processing, then start to push text across the bottom of the lens:

"Another Shocking Act of Terrorism: 15 Confirmed Deaths, Dozens Hospitalized."

My stomach clenches. I don't click through to read any more of the article. There is terrorism in this country every day, maybe that one isn't about me. The glasses have another one ready to go:

"Michaels HQ Bombed, Witnesses Report on Graphic Carnage - Body Parts Scattered Inside."

That one is less ambiguous. I pull the glasses off my face and push them away from me across the table.

"It wasn't my fault."

Buck snorts, the red growing deeper across his cheeks and up into his forehead. He smiles. "Bullshit. You are a monster."

I don't know how to explain to him that there was this girl I liked, who turned out to be a psychopath. So, I try out something I learned on TV instead, "I think I should have a lawyer."

Buck stands up from the table and knocks twice on the door. "We'll get right on that."

The twin cops with the blond mustaches open the door and enter the room. Suddenly, I'm surrounded by testosterone and fuzzy lip caterpillars.

Each of the twins grabs an arm, lifting me off my feet and dragging me out of the room. The best I can manage in protest is to be as lifeless as possible. The deadweight annoys them, and they grip my arm violently.

As I pass the threshold Buck chortles, "I'm going to run right over to my office and call the public defender for you." The twins get the joke and laugh heartily, in unison.

The hall leads to an elevator which leads to a basement which leads to a private cell with a cot and a toilet. There is no window.

Without a word, the twins release their grips and deposit me inside. There are no bars, just concrete block walls, and a plain concrete floor. The only break in the monotone is a small opening in the middle of the door, hinged from the outside. Bright light from the ceiling showers down on the little room, drenching every surface in dusty white.

The twins step out and close the door tightly.

CHAPTER EIGHTEEN

Fuzzy Caterpillars

There are no distractions in my little cell. The light never turns off or dims. The only variability in my world is the unpredictable man-child stomping around inside my cell and the flushing of the toilet. Everything else was designed for constant inertness.

Food comes through the hatch at random intervals. I've eaten what could be described as dinner twelve times and what could be described as breakfast eleven times. There is no other way to mark the time. Nothing else comes through the little hatch.

No one comes by to take away the refuse from the meals, so I stack up the trays in the corner. After all the trouble I've caused it seems like being tidy is the least I can do.

I can't sleep. Every time I close my eyes, I hear screaming. The blank walls act as the perfect screen for my mind to project my crimes onto. A wallpaper of screaming faces that I don't recognize follows me around the little box.

I wash the food down with the clean water that I scoop by hand out of the toilet. It is not as bad as I would have expected. It tastes fine. This is a suitable existence for me. I'm happy to hang out in here until some critical piece of infrastructure inside me stops working.

I have no need for companionship or stimulation. I eat, I stack trays, I poop, and I sit, I lie, I sit. I do my best not to think. Brains are dangerous instruments, and I've decided the more you can do to blunt them and mute their constant neediness, the better. My brain doesn't resist. It seems happy enough to fade away, relieved to be done with the constant worrying required by my survival.

Sometime after my eleventh "breakfast" but before my next "dinner" the door opens for the first time since it closed. It slides open soundlessly on hidden hinges while I'm in the middle of pooping out the parts of my meal my body decided were unnecessary to maintain my bleak existence.

The twins fill up the frame. They crinkle their noses, disgusted in the same way zoo-goers are disgusted watching a monkey masturbate.

"Knock on the door when you're done," one of them says as they step back out of the room, closing it behind them.

I take my time finishing up, then go sit back on the bed and watch as the skin melts off a crying face on the wall. Perhaps if I wait long enough, they will give up and leave me alone.

I am too busy slowly rotting to deal with whatever they want.

I am not going to volunteer myself for anything ever again.

My brain has thoroughly proved it cannot handle such responsibilities. The rest of my life will be spent like some sort of sea anemone, silently filtering water, satisfied by whatever happens to float past.

After a few minutes, the door swings open again, and the two fuzzy lipped caterpillars enter the room. With my new resolution to be more invertebrate in mind, I stay seated firmly on the bed.

"Let's go," one of them says.

The twins walk towards me and split off, each one grabbing an arm. I don't want to leave the room, so I go limp in their grip. It doesn't matter, they easily drag me out of the room and down the hall back to the elevator I came down in.

One of the twins passes a card through a reader as the elevator door slides shut behind us. He has to let go of me to insert the card, I set my knees to jelly and let myself fall face first all the way to the ground.

"Get up," he says toeing my ribs with one shoe.

They don't understand the non-person I have transformed myself into in the last two weeks. Sea goo doesn't stand up so neither will I. I keep my face firmly planted on the floor of the elevator.

Some grit covers my lips and makes its way into my mouth. This is how filter-feeding works. I can hear one, or both of them, sigh as the elevator drags us upward.

The door opens and they reach down, pinching under my arms, pulling me towards wherever they think it appropriate. It hurts but I don't protest. I figure the less I say, the sooner they will plant me back in my little room.

Instead, they drag me to the room I woke up in. Buck is still sitting there. It doesn't look like he ever moved. The twins deposit me in the seat across from him. I start to ooze out of the chair and onto the floor, Buck watches for a second then claps his hands loudly on the table, "Cut the shit."

Startled, I reform into a solid and sit upright. The twins close the door and take their posts behind Buck.

"Son, we have here a problem, one which we think you might be uniquely situated to help solve."

This is a confusing thing to have told to me - I can't imagine a problem I could do anything to except make more severe. Buck registers the confusion in my face and slides a pair of glasses over to me.

"Take a look," he says.

My body naturally recoils at the suggestion. The parts of my brain attracted to such things as the glasses have atrophied.

"Put them on," Buck insists, pushing them forward.

He doesn't seem to understand that sea sludge-like myself has no need for things like fancy glasses or the internet or a social conscience. Sensing my resistance, Buck nods and the twins move forward, one pinning my arms down onto the table and the other sliding the glasses over my face. They vibrate excitedly, tickling my nose, happy to discuss whatever problem Buck thinks I won't make worse.

"Death Toll From Global Famine Reaches 100 Million, Surprising Experts as It Picks Up Speed. India Joins Russia and China Threatening Preemptive Nuclear Strike if Michaels Elected."

"Michaels Promises if Elected, All Options on Table to Ensure American Supremacy: 'We Won't Be Intimidated.'"

"Son, do you know what we do here?" Buck asks peering at me through the other side of the glasses.

It seems very clear to me what they do here - this is a repository for people not suitable for the outside world. It seems like a noble and necessary cause.

All I want to do is figure out what magical combination of words will facilitate a return to my little cell. Trying to speed along the process, I nod my head up and down - "yes."

"I don't think you do," Buck says, suddenly furious. "I don't think you fucking do. I don't think you know anything. I think you're as ignorant and innocent as a little baby chimpanzee. You think running around in the woods, blowing up useless garbage makes you Bobby Badass?"

He pauses, waiting for an answer. I decide that nodding in agreement is again the straightest line between here and my room. No need to create extra conflict.

Buck stares incredulously as I nod. He exhales loudly through his mouth, dotting me with spit. The twin sentries guard the door, unmoving.

"We do things here you have no idea about. No fucking clue. Things that keep *you* safe. Things that keep the world from spinning off its axis." He pauses to let that soak in, watching for my reaction.

I can tell that his madness is manufactured. This speech is something he has done many times before.

Not convinced his words are sinking in Buck continues in a more measured tone, "I'm giving you a chance to make something of your worthless life. To live righteously and work for a cause." He pauses, sucking in a deep breath considering his words, "Now tell me, why did you blow up the campaign headquarters?"

I react to his question like a punch in the face. I don't want to be reminded of anything that happened in my life before my little white cell.

"Why'd you do it?" Buck persists.

"Because of Sam. It was Sam's idea." I respond quietly.

"What gave Sam that idea?"

I think back to her many lessons, culled from that little notebook, and struggle to come up with the connective tissue Buck seems to think is so important.

"Because of Mike Michaels?" I whisper at last.

Buck guffaws. "D'you think people like me really care about people like Mike Michaels? D'you think the people running this country are elected?"

I shrug and pull at the skin between my fingers. This conversation has become physically painful.

"People like symbols. They like the illusion of resistance. They can sit comfortably in their houses and apartments, safe and secure in the knowledge that someone is outraged. Look around, son. Things are not going well. *We* provide them with that security. As long as *someone* is outraged, the rest of the people are pacified. We are the outrage. We are their expression of rage. We give them something to unite behind – a cause, a distraction. People don't see a building in flames and run to get their gasoline, eager to get their own hands dirty. They look up from their phone and glasses for just a second and are happy to see someone outraged. They read an article and pass it on to their friends with some angry emoji attached, then they go back into their little life bubble, content to leave the hard work to us. You are just the edge of the sword. It is our job to keep the world from ending."

It seems to me the world ended a long time ago; people just haven't noticed yet.

"We know all about you. Sam and Cap work for us. Their job is to bring in fresh recruits like you, to keep our shelves of the disaffected fully stocked. They bring in the prospects and assign them test projects. You aren't the first person this week to sit on the other side of that desk and you won't be the last."

Buck leans back and drums his fingers on the armrest of his chair. He stares a hole through me and then huffs loudly. Impatiently, he checks the clock on the wall.

"Son, we need to move this along. There are two options; one you live in a black hole full of shit for the rest of your life, eating and crapping in the same room, never seeing another human being until cancer eats your guts out; or two, you go to work for us keeping the peace."

Unwittingly, Buck has thrown me a lifeline. What an easy choice! I take the glasses off and look down at my hands, playing into his drama.

"I'll take the darkroom and the cancer," I say finally with all the gravity and sincerity I can muster.

Buck sits back in his chair like I slapped him across the face.

Pushing further, I offer helpfully, hopefully, "I just think it would be best if I went back into my room and stopped bothering everyone."

Buck leans forward, dragging his chair across the floor, and drums his fingers on the table. The fuzzy caterpillar presses up into his nose as his lips curl over his teeth. He drums his fingers some more and looks over his shoulder at the twins guarding the door, nodding to each one in unison. Head tilted slightly to the left; Buck's attention turns back to me.

Suddenly the fuzzy caterpillar jumps in a sharp arc as his lips split into a deep smile. He laughs heartily and stands up from the chair. Circling the table and coming parallel with me, Buck slaps me playfully on the back.

"Ha, good one. Sorry about sticking you in that cell. We had to see what you were made of. You're not the first, but frankly, we've never seen anyone stew in there as long as you without cracking even a little. Usually, after five days they start clawing at the door and beg to be let out. You were unbreakable. We know that this test is unpleasant but it's necessary. Trust us, we've all been there."

"The boys here tell me the package Cap made for you malfunctioned, but you persevered with the plan anyway."

Buck grips my shoulder and stares down his ginger nose into my eyes. They are watery with emotion.

"You are one tough motherfucker. Together, we're going to change the world," he says as he holds my eyes for a beat and then just as quickly snaps out of it.

"The twins are going to cut you loose."

"Cut me loose?" I repeat meekly.

"That's right, son. After all is said and done, you're going to work for us. We're going to make something amazing out of you." Buck slaps his palms together and chuckles heartily. "We already have a munitions expert picked out as a partner for you. She's waiting for you out there in the field."

"The field?" The words bubble out of my mouth like a belch.

"That's right... But don't worry, you'll be monitored at all times. We'll let you know when and where to meet up with her. We're moving your territory south, back down to Florida. The sunshine state! The south has mostly been picked through, but there are some priority targets left and we've found it to be a good training ground. Something about the heat makes the people down there crazy. Understand?"

I shake my head violently, "no."

"Yes," Buck slaps me on the back, massaging my shoulders between his thick, freckled hands.

He chuckles and twists a thumb painfully into a tendon connecting my shoulder to my neck. The twins laugh too. Everyone is laughing and rubbing my back and laughing. Fuzzy caterpillars are jumping excitedly all over the room.

All of a sudden, I am up off my feet again, a twin on each arm, leading me out the door. One of them slips a new backpack across my shoulders, and as if carried by some unseen wave, I am pushed down the hall. From behind me, Buck calls, "Hunker down for a few days. Relax a bit. We'll find you."

The wave continues up a staircase, through a door, and into an alley where the twins drop me off. One of them winks and hands me a new pair of glasses.

"These are the newest generation - they respond to brain vibrations. Oh, and don't forget to vote."

And with that, the door is closed, and I'm alone in an alley I've never seen. The sunlight is weak and disorienting. It is cold, so very cold.

CHAPTER NINETEEN

Civic Duty

I couldn't go back to my sad little apartment. It took me two days to make my way to the family camp, to the Coop. The backpack the twins strapped on me was heavy. When I opened it, all I found were Nacho flavored Go-Bars. I spent the journey slowly crumbling the bars in my pockets, dropping the pieces behind me. I don't think any of the animals that aren't hibernating will be hungry enough to eat up my trail.

The house has been boarded up for years, ever since the little microbes living in amongst the waves made a new home in my father.

I find it still boarded up tightly, along with all the other houses in the neighborhood. Oceanfront living isn't as in demand as it once was. The water is higher than I remember as a kid. Waves lap lazily at the now rotting shingles that encircle the bottom of the porch. Walking around the house,

I find where one of the boards was pulled off a window. I climb through the opening and step into the old house.

The floors creak underfoot and little beams of grey light from pinhole openings throughout the living room penetrate the blackness just enough to keep me from tripping over the discarded clothes that litter the floor. Someone or someones have been squatting here. It smells like they have continued to use the old plumbing well past its useful life.

I unlock the slider that faces the ocean and push through a piece of rotted plywood. The porch sags around the water as the ocean continues to slowly consume all the land that used to be dry.

A breeze gusts up out at sea, kicking up whitecaps. It makes me shiver. The glasses in my pocket mimic my movements and shudder along. I put them on and a new headline springs up immediately.

"As Votes are Tallied, World on Edge - American Election Pushes World Towards Brink of Nuclear Showdown."

A new application opens blacking out the ocean. Red text scrolls across my twitching pupils. "Welcome to Civic Duty. Voter Polls are Now Open. Blink Now to Activate Voter Registration."

I blink.

The glasses hum again, tickling the bridge of my nose as they process my identity.

"Registration Approved. Blink Now to Enter Voting Booth."

I blink again.

"Welcome to the Voting Booth. You Have Two Choices for President. Blink Once to Vote."

I blink.

The glasses start humming, interpreting my brain waves. What truly amazing technology, finally a machine that can tell me what I'm thinking.

"You Have Voted for Michael Michaels. Blink Twice to Confirm."

That sounds about right. Blink-blink.

"Vote Confirmed. Thank You for Fulfilling Your Patriotic Duty. Blink Now to Enter the Rest of the Ballot."

I pull the glasses off my face and toss them into the waves at the bottom of the porch. The glasses light up angrily, vibrating against the rocks. Snail food.

I sit on the slanted floor; the waters lapping at my feet and watch the ocean eat everything around me.

Eat, ocean, eat. Yum.

*   *   *

Author Bio

J esse is a writer living in southern Maine. Anarchy is his second novel. His first novel, Dead Cats and Other Reflections on Parenthood was selected by Publishers Weekly as a semi-finalist for their 2017 Booklife Prize.